SHORT STORIES

FANTASY, TIME TRAVEL, SCI FI, ADVENTURE AND MORE

William Neve

Outskirts Press, Inc.
Denver, Colorado

Short Stories - Fantasy, Time Travel, Sci Fi, Adventure and More

Outskirts Press, Inc.
http://www.outskirtspress.com

ISBN: 978-1-4327-2214-2

Outskirts Press and the "OP" logo are trademarks belonging to Outskirts Press, Inc.

PRINTED IN THE UNITED STATES OF AMERICA

ADVENTURES
IN TIME

CHAPTER 1
LEARNING TO TIME TRAVEL

Bill Snow, at the time of this story, was in his sixties. He had known for years that he had out- of -body experiences. He was very conservative with its use however, since on one occasion when he was traveling out of the solar system at an incredible rate of speed, that he had to force himself to wake up to get back. His daughter, Nicole, told him in confidence, that she was having out- of- body experiences, and wondered if she was losing her mind. He told her that her ability must have been inherited from him, because he also had the experiences. They decided to test their abilities by meeting together, at a designated place, in out- of- body form. They met as planned and were amazed at what they could hear, see and travel to with their bodies safely home in their beds. In a meeting, they discussed the possibility of time- travel. That evening, they got together, in out- of- body, and tried to travel to the past. They could feel the ripples in the time fabric, but fell short of making the jump. There was no more talk of time- travel for quite a while, until Nicole discovered that her niece, Tori, Bill's other daughter's girl, was also having out- of- body experiences. To their surprise, she knew of their attempt to time- travel and thought they didn't have enough combined power to do it. She thought if the three of them got together, they might be able to make it happen. After much discussion and concern, they decided to try a trip back in time to the French Revolution where their ancestors had lived. To their amazement, this time it worked, and not only that, they were in full body and could be seen, feel, hear and possibly die. They had to be very careful.

CHAPTER 2
A VISIT TO THE FRENCH REVOLUTION

They arrived in Paris in the year 1789; Madame Guillotine was busy chopping off the heads of the Aristocracy. Madame Lafarge was busy knitting her accounts. Bill told the girls that their ancestor, a Marquis, could be in line for execution.

After a thorough search, they found the Marquis. Bill had to subdue a guard, who was half asleep. They talked to the Marquis, who was able to understand English. They explained to the Marquis that they were his future descendants. He didn't believe a word they said but would gratefully accept any help they could give him. He was let out using the keys taken from the guard and they found their way outside. A horse and carriage nearby was confiscated and they sped away. Driving through the square, they heard the cheers as another Aristocrat lost his head. The Marquis directed them out of the city to the country side where he had friends that would help him to get out of France. He wondered how and why they engineered his escape. They told him they weren't positive themselves, but it was important to them, they being his descendants, and because they wouldn't exist in the future if he didn't continue to live and have children. He told them that he didn't believe what they were telling him, but that he was grateful for them saving his life. Having no reason to stay any longer, they put their heads together and were projected back in time. Back to the year 2007 they congratulated each other and resolved to do it again.

CHAPTER 3
ENLIGHTENMENT

The three of them got together again and decided to test their time- travel abilities. As before, in out of body mode, they put their combined power into traveling to the future. Arriving in the future they found themselves trapped in a huge hall. The walls rose one hundred feet or more and were made of gleaming alabaster. At the end of the hall was a raised judge's bench with three persons seated there. They approached the bench and were addressed by the central person. She told them that they had brought them there to stop their irresponsible travels in time and that they had accidentally discovered a way to time- travel by using their combined mental power. In this future time, the year 2500, she told them that they had evolved genetically, providing them the capability in the same way, except that they could do it singularly. She continued to tell them of the dangers of traveling in the past and changing something that would change things in the future. She told them that their advanced technology allowed them to monitor any breach of the time continuum and that they followed their journey to the French Revolution and luckily no problem was caused because the Marquis's friends were there to free him also. The horse and carriage you confiscated was left there by them to aid in the escape. Finally, she told them that they were the Time- Travel Federation Tribunal and that she was Madam President. Their fate was going to be decided by the Tribunal. Before any decision was to be made, she explained that their ability to time- travel is possible by utilizing brain waves. The power of brain waves is infinite. She also explained that out- of- body experience is possible by using brain waves. Additionally the genes from your lineage have begun to evolve, making time- travel possible. She told them because of the prior mentioned dangers of time-travel, the Tribunal has created laws governing time travel. They were told not to underestimate their position if they were left here, trapped in the future, their bodies in the past would succumb. She told them that they have one option, they can join the Federation and as members they would be implanted with a cell sized micro chip that would transcend to their bodies and permit the monitoring of their position at all times. Their responsibilities would be as follows:

1. Obey all time-travel laws
2. Keep all information and existence of the Federation secret
3. Agree to accept a mission as deemed necessary by the Tribunal

They agreed to join the Federation and were immediately implanted and released from the hall. Back in their bodies, they wondered what they had got themselves into.

CHAPTER 4
FIRST MISSION ASSIGNMENT

The three of them met again to consider another venture in time. After falling asleep, they all met, out- of- body, and concentrated on a trip to the future. Instead they landed in the big hall again. The Tribunal was in session, and again Madam President spoke telling them that if they hadn't realized it by now they should know that any attempt to travel in time will bring them right there for approval. She told them that they were about to get in touch with them anyway and that they had a mission for their consideration.

She told them that any missions they would require would be very critical and should be handled by persons from the past before any travel in time. Persons with an excellent knowledge of history, like them. To further explain, she told them that Mankind's ability to time- travel started around the year 2480; however, some people acquired the ability earlier. They hoped that the three of them were the very earliest. Later they realized that controls would be necessary to stop any changes, as explained before. Prior to implementing controls, many rogue time travelers made changes to suit themselves. The changes they made caused many parallel universes to be affected. The Tribunal has developed technology to monitor these universes, but as yet have no ability to travel to them.

The mission that the Tribunal has for the three was to go back in time and explore any changes that they can detect from known historical knowledge. Their first mission will be to start with the year 1950, if they decide to accept.

They all decided to accept the mission and immediately arrived back in the year 1950. They witnessed some incredible changes; the Nazi flag was coupled everywhere with the American flag. As they walked down Main St. of their town, they noticed people greeting each other with Nazi salutes. They stopped at the library and delved into the history books. They discovered that Germany did not lose the Second World War. They were able to settle a peaceful cease fire to their benefit. Nicole went out to ask people in the street what had happened. Meanwhile, from the history books, they learned that the Nazis became a third party in the American system of democracy. They found no mention, in any books, about a Holocaust. Upon leaving the library they were stopped by an official looking person who asked for their papers. They said that they didn't have any papers. He advised them to go to city hall and get registered, and be sure to indicate if they were Jewish. At that point, Nicole returned from the street and told them of her disbelief at what she had learned. She told them that Hitler was alive; he has had a child with Eva Braun. He is controlling Europe with an iron fist. His territory contains part of France, Russia and all territories with German heritage. All Nazi buildings bombed by the Allies were restored, paid for by the Allies. Germany is a super power and enjoys considerable influence world wide.

They tried to end the mission by going back to their time, but instead they were brought back to the great hall. Addressing the Tribunal, they related all they had learned. They asked why they weren't witnessing a corresponding change in the future. They were told that it is manifested in a parallel universe. The Tribunal told them that they would decide on a course of action and would call them soon for a follow- up mission. They went back to their time and pondered in disbelief at what they had learned.

CHAPTER 5
A FOLLOW UP MISSION

As promised, a person sent by the Tribunal, appeared in Bill's dream and introduced himself as Jobe. He told him that their next mission, as a follow up to the last mission, would be for them to go to the year 1943, the 16th of October; Nazi Germany is their destination. He went on to explain that they are to stop a rogue time- traveler from the year 2200. His name is Hans Shicklgruber, a descendant of Adolph Hitler's. Hans was able to get plans of the Atomic bomb to Adolph Hitler. Because of that change of event in time Germany was able to develop the bomb about the same time as the USA. They made cease fire settlements with the Allies, thus keeping the Third Reich intact .

In the future, the Third Reich exists in a parallel universe. Your mission is to intercept Hans and destroy the Atomic Bomb plans. The Tribunal is confident that if the objective is achieved, then the parallel universe will revert back as it should be.

The three got together to decide if they wanted to accept the mission. They all agreed that the assignment was out of their league and probably should be handled by professionals. They had no idea of how to find Hans and because he was a time- traveler also, he could spot them easily. Additionally, none of them could speak German. They decided to go to the Tribunal to present their case. They gathered as usual and traveled to the great hall. They approached the Tribunal and presented their concerns to Madam President. She agreed with their concerns and offered a compromise. She told them that they had developed a device that would tell them when they were near a time-traveler. It would indicate the direction and pulse faster as the traveler got closer. She told them that if they could indicate where Hans was, his exact location and the exact time, they could take care of him remotely. The three agreed to try and find him, whereupon they were immediately sent to Nazi Germany in the year 1943. When they arrived, the device started pulsing and was getting stronger. They were at a train station in Berlin. As a train coming their way got closer, the device pulsed faster; Hans was definitely on that train. As people got off of the train, they noticed a slight man, with a mustache, carrying a briefcase. He started toward them, then turned and ran in the opposite direction. Some- how he spotted them; they noted the exact location and time. They hung around for a while and noticed a lot of distressed, beaten down people being loaded into a freight car like cattle. They were disgusted, but had to act nonchalant or be questioned.

Later, another train was coming in the distance; the device started pulsing again. They noticed the same man getting off when the train pulled in. This time, he called some uniformed men with swastika arm bands and pointed at them. They noted the exact time and the exact location and banded together for transport. They were transported to the Tribunal in the future. Jobe was there; he told them that they had Hans pinpointed. He had cleverly eluded them by going back and forth in time. That's why you reported seeing him twice. Jobe said that he would take it from there, and that they will take drastic measures that won't be pretty. They arrived back at home relieved that the mission was over.

CHAPTER 6
STOCK MARKET CRASH

A message came from Jobe to Bill, that a mission was needed to stop a time- traveler from changing his ancestor's misfortune during the Stock Market Crash of 1929. They all got together again and traveled to the great hall. Facing the Tribunal, they were told by Madam President that a renegade time- traveler had changed one of the results of the 1929 Stock Market Crash. She suspected it may be an ancestor of a man called, Adam White; Adam killed himself by jumping off the roof of a ten story hotel after the crash. They were told to go there and stop him in any way they could. They were sent to the time of October 28, 1929. They found themselves in a hotel off of Wall St. in New York City. They checked with the hotel clerk and determined that an Adam White had signed in, but his key was missing from the rack, indicating that he was out. Thinking that the renegade might try to contact Adam in his hotel room, they entered the room and added a remote microphone to the radio.

They went through all his papers and saw that Adam was buying inflated stock on margin; it looked like the renegade was going to convince Adam to sell everything before October 29, 1929 when the Stock Market would crash. They left the room before Adam came back and returned to the adjacent room which they were occupying. Later, Adam came into his room and turned on the radio to listen to the stock market reports. A while later they heard a knock at Adams door and a man entered. They heard loud arguing and what sounded like some pushing around. Taking this apparent opportunity, they interrupted the radio program using the remote mike, to announce that people should be on the lookout for a crazy man who is telling people that he is their ancestor and to sell their valuable stock; he is trying to bilk people out of their money. A fight broke out in the other room, and then it got real quiet. We learned later that Adam grabbed a knife during their fight and killed the renegade. The next day when the stock market crashed, Adam realized that he had killed his time traveling ancestor and had lost all his money just as his ancestor had predicted. All this was too much for him; he went up to the roof of the hotel and jumped.

The three of them appeared before the Tribunal and were congratulated on the success of their mission. They were told that the identity of the renegade was not important; with his death the problem is solved.

CHAPTER 7
THE LOST DUTCHMAN'S GOLD

Bill, Tori and Nicole got together again to discuss plans for time- travel. Nicole mentioned that her uncle Bob had built a home in Arizona near Gold Canyon and that the canyon got its name from the story of the lost Dutchman's gold mine. As the story goes, back in the nineteenth century a gold miner from Holland, spent many years searching for gold. Past evidence indicated that from his years of buying supplies that he had struck it rich. No one has ever discovered his strike, if he had one. Many people over the years have tried to find his mine. Phony maps supposedly showing the location of the mine have been sold to gullible people. Nicole suggested that they go back and follow him; they might get lucky.

They traveled to the Tribunal to ask for approval. After listening to their plans, Madam President asked them what they would do with the gold if they found it. They explained that they would turn it over to the government and that any amount that fell to them would be given to charity after their expenses. Using conventional travel, they drove out to Gold Canyon Arizona as guests of uncle Bob. They could not discuss their real intentions but told Bob that they would like to tour the area and do some old- time prospecting for gold. He laughed and wished them lots of luck. They got together and time- traveled to the year 1850. They talked to prospectors and asked if they had heard of a prospector from Holland. They told them that they had seen the crazy old man and that he's been in and out of the old canyon for years without an ounce of gold. He buys supplies on each trip with old dollar bills he must have had for years, he's been in there for days, but he should be coming out before too long for supplies. The three of them rented horses and with an ample supply of food and water they went into the canyon. They explored the canyon all day long and never saw any sign of the Dutchman. They returned the horses and went back to their time. In their time they decided to go camping in the Gold Canyon. With ample supplies, they drove to the far end of the canyon and prepared to stay the night. They slept and soon were in out- of- body mode. In this mode they could penetrate any cave or hiding place. They probed all around and finally they found it, the Dutchman's gold was in there; bags and bags of gold were everywhere. They went back to their campsite and woke up too excited to sleep. In the morning they drove to the place where they saw the mine and tried to find a way in. Examining the canyon wall very closely they noticed a huge jagged rock section that was hinged. They pulled it open and went in to view the gold but to their surprise the gold was gone. Somebody had beat them to it, but how? They drove back to Bob's house wondering what had happened.

CHAPTER 8
THE MISSING GOLD

They didn't have to wonder long about what had happened to the missing gold. Jobe visited Bill in a dream and told him that they were going to be asked to accept a secret mission related to the missing gold; he said that only Madam President and he would know of the mission. They believed that someone high up in their government may be involved in the missing gold. In the year 2500, gold is very rare and has increased in value to the equivalent of five thousand dollars an ounce. The Dutchman's gold would be worth billions. It is believed that a traitor to the Time Federation monitored your journey and followed you to your find. We believe the traitor hid the gold in an area known only to him. They were told that their mission, if they accept it, would be to identify the traitor and to locate the gold. They activated their time- traveler locator device to help them in the search.

They were advised that no further contact must be made to the Tribunal, if they decided to accept, they were to just go ahead with the mission and report only when they have completed the mission. Bill explained the visit by Jobe and their commitment if they accept it. They all accepted and Bill was very proud of the two girls for their courage.

They were already in Arizona so they time- traveled back to the time when they noticed the missing gold. They rented horses and went back to the location of the gold mine. They pulled open the hinged jagged rock and entered the mine, there was no sign of any gold, but they did find a dead body, to their amazement. Confused they left the body there and headed back to turn in the horses they had rented. They asked people if anything strange had happened recently. They said yes, a bunch of wild Mexicans came through loaded with gold and spent a fortune in liquor, food and entertainment and looked like they struck it rich. They told the three of them that they must have been up to no good because some of us who speak Spanish, overheard them talking about killing a man who tried to hire them to transport some gold. On top of that the old Dutchman showed up talking crazy and left town for good.

They traveled to the tribunal and reported that the gold was spent mostly in Mexico and the person that didn't show up for his government job was the traitor. He was killed by his own greed. Madam President told them that they knew who he was and understand what happened to the gold. They were congratulated for solving a century's long mystery and doing a great job in their mission. Back at uncle Bob's, they told him that they had no luck at prospecting and were going home.

CHAPTER 9
A LOOK AT THE FUTURE

Jobe came to Bill in a dream and told him that the Tribunal had a surprise for them. He got them all together and they traveled to the great hall and found it filled with people that were applauding as they came in. They were quite surprised and approached the Tribunal quite dumbfounded.

Madam President welcomed them and told them that because of their successful efforts, all known renegade time- travelers have been brought to justice. She told them that the Tribunal and the citizens of the Earth Federation were here to reward them for their achievement. She presented each of them the top Medal Of Time Travel award. She told them that because of their courageous efforts, they have earned the complete trust of the Tribunal and because of that trust they will be allowed to look at the future, their year 2500. It was revealed to them that because this year 2500 was the year time- travel was achieved; no future time- travel is possible beyond this date. The future beyond this date doesn't exist yet in our universe; however we are confident that the future beyond our time does exist in some parallel universe. The Tribunal has not solved the way to travel to other universes.

After greeting many Earth Federation top officials and members of the Tribunal, the great doors to the hall were opened welcoming them to Earth Federation City. They were awed by the spectacle, buildings rose thousands of feet through the clouds, there were no roads. People traveled in vehicles that defied gravity; many individuals were hovering in air traveling by themselves. The air seemed clean and refreshing; all around were parks and green plush foliage. Their guide, Jobe, handed them antigravity belts and showed them how to use them. There was no traffic control because the belts had anti-collision capability. Jobe told them that the entire Earth's people belong to the Earth Federation Government. robots keep the peace and police everything; any breach of the law is dealt with very quickly. The robots report to the Tribunal and serve mankind in many ways. They are used in manufacturing for just about everything. They can't dream, however, lacking brain waves and as a result they can't time- travel. They were told that they have developed antigravity technology; all vehicles use this for travel. All energy is from fusion, fossil fuel has been outlawed. The global warming problem has been cured. A population problem still exists but may be cured with space travel. Colonies have been established in our solar system that are being populated aggressively. En-vironmentally controlled cities have been built on Saturn's moon Titan and Jupiter's moons Europa and Ganymede.

The Milky Way, our galaxy, is 80,000 light years wide making exploration somewhat limited. The Earth Federa-tion with the Time Travel Tribunal is working on the tech-nology to travel through Worm Holes in space. The technology, if successful, would permit traveling anywhere in the universe in zero time. For example, Andromeda our nearest galaxy is 2.4 million light years away; travel to this galaxy would be possible through a Worm Hole in space time. The three heroes were invited to a huge banquet in their honor, which they enjoyed completely. Later, back in their time, they had medals hanging from their necks that they could not share with anyone.

A DARK
MATTER

CHAPTER 1
DISCOVERY

John Royal was a Physics Professor at M. I. T. in Cambridge, Massachusetts. He earned his PHD there and decided at the time to remain there teaching. He left the Institute to work with a staff of scientists on the newly built European 100 mile Cyclotron. He was very interested in the discoveries that the new equipment would reveal. The equipment was predicted to create conditions as they were at the start of the Big Bang, the beginning of the universe. With the initial runs of the equipment many new particles were created that lasted only an instant in time. Many hours were needed to confirm the findings which took up the time of several Scientists. On one shift, that was run by John, he noticed some new material that he could not identify. It had weird qualities, faster than light speed and not affected by gravity. His supervisor studied his results and disagreed with his findings. He told him to forget it and work in another area. John did not follow his instructions and instead worked on ways to capture the material. After many tries, he finally managed to capture the material using a crystal container. When his supervisor found out that he had not done anything else for days, he told John to go back to teaching and fired him. This action delivered a blow to his status and reputation. John left Europe in anger and threatened to get even. He set up his own lab in his home in Massachusetts and stayed in seclusion for weeks. All this time, he was working with the material he confiscated and was discovering what it really was. He learned how to handle it and marveled at its weird behavior. He discovered that this material was the cold dark matter that makes up most of the universe. Also the material radiates dark energy that is unaffected by gravity and is causing the universe to continue to expand at an incredible rate. He found that the dark energy would release instantly if not controlled. It could be controlled if the release rate is held to a rate that would keep the energy in the immediate vicinity.

John devised a crystal box tied to a belt that would contain the material and could be worn around his waist. By employing crystal valves, operated by code initiated electronics; he could turn the energy off and on. The weird affect of the energy release was to change time for the wearer of the belt. For every second passing outside the energy's influence, the wearer would have 20 minutes to maneuver. In effect everything would be motionless as seen by the wearer of the belt.

John realized the great power that was at his disposal. He decided to store the belt in a secure place where nobody could find it. A good thing he did because right at that time the CIA was at his door. They confronted John and asked him, what he had done with the dark material he stole. It turn out that further study by his supervisor concluded that John was right about the discovery of dark matter. After a search of John's house, they found his notes and some dark material, enough to convict him. The belt was not found. Ultimately John was convicted of stealing valuable material and was sentenced to five years in federal prison, parole after two.

CHAPTER 2
THE DARK SIDE

The only satisfaction John had upon entering prison was the fact that his former supervisor was fired from his job. The CIA was never able to do anything with John's cryptic notes and dark matter. John made a lot of friends in prison. The inmates highly respected him and wanted to be part of any endeavor he got into. John learned a lot from his friends and established contacts that would come in handy later. John came out of prison two years later and was on parole. He was changed, no longer trusting and quite ready to do anything to benefit himself. He realized that the CIA was following him and devised ways to throw them off of his trail. He managed to get back to his secure hiding place and put on the belt. He switched it on, regulated the flow and noted that it worked perfectly. Call it power crazy or just madness but he headed for the CIA office to exact revenge. With the switch on, he entered their office, unseen. Everyone was motionless; he went into the secret files and removed all the documents. He saw no one around and switched to real time, then he locked the file room door. He proceeded to send sensitive documents to the FBI, politicians and citizens being scrutinized by the CIA, using the Fax machine. He then opened the door, switched the belt on, and walked out of the office in hardly any real time. The repercussions of his actions caused panic in the CIA and many heads began to roll. The task was so easy, it heightened his power craze. The CIA never found out what hit them.

John was still young and with his worldly good looks, women fell easy prey to his advances. He soon discovered he needed money to keep up his life style. So he set out to rob as many banks as he could. It was so easy it was ridiculous. He just walked into the banks with the belt switched on and filled his satchel and walked out. In a short time he had all the money he would ever need. He left a lot of bank managers thoroughly confused and the authorities dumb founded. His visits to diamond stores were even more rewarding.

CHAPTER 3
A NEW LIFE

With the parole board on his back, John decided it was time to get rid of his old identity and to assume a new one. To live his life style, out in the open, he would have to kill John Royal. With the help of his friends, he staged a car wreck using a dead body supplied by his friends. With John's car used in the wreck and the body burned beyond recognition, the coroner had to conclude that John had died. Through connections that he learned about in prison, he paid a plastic surgeon to alter his features. From other sources, he obtained ID papers, a passport and a driver's license, showing his identity as Robert Heller. He proceeded to bank funds using his new identity, and to wire them overseas to France, Spain, Switzerland, and Germany. In each country, he sought well protected castles, ones that had the particular fortifications he required.

In each country, he enjoyed his life style of wine, women and song. He became very famous as the most eligible bachelor abroad. He had unusual good luck at the gambling casinos, mostly because of his unseen visits to set things to his advantage. Having trusted friends, with vested interest at each castle, made it very easy for him to come and go across Europe as he pleased.

Key people, in each castle, procured what he needed, when he needed it. He set up a network of computer experts that could hack into any sensitive area he desired. He made many friends whom he helped with financing for ventures like, hotels, restaurants and commercial business.

CHAPTER 4
PAYBACK

As Robert Heller, and his ability to control time, he was able to do good or evil. Feeling some remorse for his past deeds, he decided it was payback time. His network informed him that terrorists were planning to bomb the US Embassy in France. They were not going to harm his native land, if he could prevent it. Using his network knowledge, he arrived at the terrorist's camp. He saw that they were all set to go. The explosives were in a Red Cross van. He switched the belt on and entered the van; he switched the belt off, defused the bomb, switched back on and left the van. He contacted the Embassy and the authorities; he told them of the plot leaving his name for credibility. The terrorists killed themselves when the plot failed. For his effort, he was praised and given a commendation by the US government. However, he had identified himself as an enemy of AL-Qaida. He told his network to be on guard.

As he thought might happen, all four of his castles were attacked at once. Some of his Castles that he thought were very secure were breached. However, AL-Qaida was defeated at each place. Robert personally took care of the one in France. He was there and switched the belt on, stopping at each terrorist and switching off to kill them. He repeated the procedure until all were dead. He did lose several of his people who died protecting his castles. Their families were well taken care of.

CHAPTER 5
A NEW ALLIANCE

After his fight with Al-Qaida, he received praise all over the world. England stepped forward and offered him Knighthood. He gratefully accepted and as "Sir Robert", he acquired a fifth castle in the UK, which was befitting his title. His Coat of Arms had a gold sword on it. He was soon beset with many loyal followers to mind his castle.

Everyone knew he had some strange power but they would never guess that he was actually, John Royal, the criminal.

He had many loving women who came forward with their offerings. One red headed Irish beauty, named Bridget, really caught his fancy. She got real close to him and after a night of love, she asked him about the belt that he wore around his waist. He answered by saying that it was the power of his Knighthood. While he slept, she slipped the belt off of him and brought it to her father who was in the IRA. He told her that he couldn't get it to work without the correct code to open it. She brought it back and put it on him, just in time, as he was waking up. She teased him a lot about the belt, she told him it was ugly and did nothing for him. Finally, he gave in; he sat her on his lap and turned it on. She was shocked at what she saw and speechless; however she managed to remember the code. A few nights later, after Sir Robert fell asleep; she took the belt to her father. She gave him the code and he quickly put on the belt and turned on the box. He opened the valve wide, a costly error, and was swept into oblivion with his daughter and everything around him. When Sir Robert woke up and noticed his belt was gone, he went looking for Bridget. He went to her father's place and saw the devastation. He realized that she had taken the belt and used it incorrectly. With a broken heart, he vowed never to trust a woman again.

CHAPTER 6
NO MATTER

With the belt gone, Sir Robert was out of his power. He wasn't feeling good and was experiencing pain all over. A doctor's visit and later many x-rays and second opinions revealed that he had incurable bone cancer. He was given six months to live and used it giving to charity and causes he believed in.

He set up an organization to combat Al-Qaida using all his resources. Before he died, he pulled together all the information on his invention pertaining to dark matter and directed it to be delivered to a person that he had selected upon his death. The information also contained his real identity. The problem of obtaining dark matter he left to his successor.

PORTALS TO THE UNIVERSE

CHAPTER 1
A PORTAL TO MIRACUS

In the year 2500 Astronomers discovered a Worm Hole in space located near Pluto in the Kuiper Belt. Since then, engineers have been working on the design of a Gravitational Wave Receiver/ Transmitter, GWRT. Scientists have known for years that passage through a Worm Hole tunnel to another part of the universe is theoretically possible. However, the exact Kerr solutions of the Einstein Field Equations indicate the tunnel is very unstable. The slightest perturbation could seal it off and convert it into a singularity where nothing can pass. Passing through a Worm Hole with a, GWRT, would record and playback the gravitational waves thereby canceling the disturbances before the tunnel could collapse and be destroyed.

In 2507 the device was completed and looked very promising. Subsequently, the latest in space ships was selected for the task of going to the Worm Hole. A crew from the NASA Space Center was organized for the journey. A robot was constructed to be used to test the new GWRT. It will be carried in the space ship and released at the proper time. Because of the vast distance to Pluto, approximately 4.9 hours light speed, it takes 3 years to make the trip using conventional engines.

However, a new Anti-Matter Engine will be used that should reduce the time to six months. The spaceship was given the name, Columbus, for its purpose of exploration.

In May of 2507 the space ship took off from Cape Canaveral on its way to Pluto.

The crew, Captain Harm Knowles, Co-Pilot Josh Edwards and three crew members, Nicole Snow, John Howe and Mary Englehart were well trained and eager to go. Nicole being the expert on the, GWRT, was responsible for the operation of it and the robot carrying it. John was the Navigator and Mary overall operation. Supplies were on board for two years and back- up systems available for all essential equipment.

The flight was fairly trouble free, the crew keeping busy with routine work and the use of exercise equipment that was on board. Finally they arrived at Pluto and placed the ship in orbit with its moon Charon.

Pluto is very small about .19 times the diameter of Earth. Its period around the sun is 247.7 years. It consists of water, methane, ammonia and ice. It has one moon, Charon.

Charon is .4 times the diameter of the Earths moon. Its orbit around Pluto is 6.39 days.

With out any delay, the crew pushed the robot into service. Nicole gave her ok and sped it on its way. It entered the worm hole and disappeared instantly. Earth was sent a message that the robot went through. The robot finally returned, its appearance proving the success of the, GWRT. With the robot back on board, the pictures it had taken were down loaded and sent to Earth. The pictures revealed that it had entered the Andromeda Galaxy in the outer arm of the spiral. The Milky Way Galaxy was clearly shown. This brought a big cheer from the crew for a monumental achievement.

Andromeda and the Milky Way are part of the local group which lies on the edge of the Virgo Super Cluster. Andromeda is the closest galaxy to the Milky Way at a distance of 2.4 million miles. Both galaxies are heading toward each other and in the far future will collide.

The pictures also revealed that the robot had arrived into a solar system similar to earths.

The Captain decided to follow through with the planned

scenario to take the ship into the worm hole. Entering into the tunnel the GWRT turned on automatically.

Almost immediately, they came out into Andromeda. Captain Knowles decided to orbit a planet that looked similar to earth. It was smaller than earth but had enough breathable air to sustain life. Josh and Nicole stayed aboard the ship while the Captain, John and Mary took the shuttle to the planets surface. Upon landing they discovered a civilization that had been battered badly. Ruins were all around and people in disarray. They stopped by wounded people and noted that they were similar to earth people. They used their computer language converter to converse with the wounded. One individual, who looked like he was in charge, asked who they were and where they had come from. They told him that their space ship was in orbit around their planet. They offered to help in any way they could. He immediately called his command central and told them that the foreign space ship in orbit was friendly and to cancel attack plans. They breathed a sigh of relief and contacted their ship to send needed medical supplies. They were invited to the command center and told the present situation on the planet. They related that they were a peace loving planet and that a warring neighbor planet had invaded them and were attempting to annihilate them and steal all their scientific knowledge. They knew about the worm hole in space and hoped the invaders did not. They were caught off guard by the invaders, but they will have a surprise coming when they return. It forced the development of weapons of mass destruction that is way beyond the capability of the invaders. The Captain was told to advise their ship of the situation and to be on alert. They told the earth crew that their planet was called Carthe, which translates to, Paradise; the warring planet was called, Darka, which translates to all powerful. They explained that their galaxy, which you call, Andromeda, is called Miracus, after one of their ancient gods. The Cartheons were told that the visitors were from a planet called Earth, in a galaxy called, The Milky Way. They entered the worm hole on an exploring mission, hoping to find other people in the universe. Earth is a peaceful planet, although it has had its problems in the past. With robotic technology everything is kept peaceful. The leader and commander of the planet introduced himself as Vel.

The visitors were invited to stay and exchange technology. They dined on exotic food, not available on earth. They were treated to scintillating beverages that enhanced their senses. At one interval, they took the shuttle back to the ship, to allow Josh and Nicole a trip to the planet for introduction and hospitality. They were amazed at the Cartheons ability to recover and fortify for a possible attack, which could come at any time. As was expected, an alert came through that the Darkas had left their planet in force and were coming fast. The Captain and the crew wished the Cartheons good luck and prepared to leave. They had no weapons and had no choice but to leave. The Cartheons told them that they knew where they were located in their galaxy and solar system and hoped they could return the visit, after they defeated the Darkas.The Captain and the crew shuttled up to the ship, just as all hell broke loose. It looked like the Darkas were getting annihilated. Unfortunately the Darkas spotted the ship and started for it. The Captain ordered the ship back to the worm hole and entered with the Darkas ship not far behind. The earth ship got through using the, GWRT; however the Darkas ship got crushed to oblivion, as the worm hole closed forever.

The ship returned to its orbit of Pluto. They sent a message to earth, down loading all that happened and the technological data they had learned from the Cartheons. They were told, five hours later, to come back to earth; a job well done, beyond anyone's expectations. On the six month trip back to earth, they pondered the possibility that the Cartheons might find another way to short cut travel, through the

Universe. Their advanced technology, which they shared with them, indicated a definite possibility.

Captain Knowles disclosed to the crew a conversation he had with Vel about establishing a portal from their planet to earth. With construction of portals on each planet, based on technology, discovered by scientists on Carthe, instant travel would be possible across the 2.4 million miles from galaxy to galaxy. He told the crew that the design and data was included in the downloaded information sent to earth. Vel had told the captain that they would be working on the portal after the defeat of the Darkans and their re-build phase.

CHAPTER 2
A PORTAL FROM EARTH TO CARTHE

When the Columbus spaceship finally landed back on earth, a hugh celebration was conducted honoring the crew. Captain Knowles was promoted to General. Nicole Snow was appointed Science Advisor to the World President. John, Josh and Mary were rewarded with promotions and remuneration. General Knowles was convinced of the importance of building the portal. He and Nicole convinced the president that the top secret work should start. In 2508, the funding was provided for the project and it started immediately.

Nicole Snow was appointed to head the project. She employed the necessary scientists, engineers and workers to accomplish the task. The theory that the Cartheons had developed, was to build a device with the necessary power, which would cause a rift in space time. A tunnel would be formed, emanating from the portal, which would flop around trying to find a way to connect to the universe, but not having the power at that end to penetrate anywhere. With a portal, in this case in Carthe; it could latch on and create a passage. A craft, similar to the one with GWRT would be required to hold the tunnel open. Only one craft would be used, thereby preventing any simultaneous passage from each end, which could be disastrous. During the design phase, it was realized, that specialized and intricate tooling would be required in the portal's manufacture. Also, a new material would be required to withstand the enormous power and stress during the portal's operation.

Finally, two years later, the project was completed and ready for trial. When the power was first turned on, it shook the building like an earthquake, but settled down to a steady hum. The project was an apparent success. A rift in space time was created and after a time the tunnel locked on and stabilized. The craft was available using a robot for the first run. The craft was sent through the portal as everyone was gripped with anxiety, hoping that all the work wasn't for nothing. Nicole, the General, the original crew, scientists, engineers and not least of all the President was witnessing the event. The site for the event was an undisclosed area of New England. All of a sudden, the portal activated, indicating that the craft was coming back. It came through the portal with an almost magical appearance. The robot was not driving the craft; instead it was Vel, from Carthe, with a big smile on his face. Their reunion was met with cheers and celebration equal to none before. Vel was introduced to the President and others. Everyone had many questions for Vel and with an interpreter, he was eager to answer.

Vel told them of the defeat of the Darkans; it was catastrophic, but necessary. Their name was changed from Darkan to Menas, or in English, from All Powerful to All Humble. Their society has been completely changed. Robots were put in charge of their security and police. They are now a very peaceful planet; a planet they are nurturing as a sister or brother.

They exchanged information on the design of the portals; as a result improvements will be made at each end. Vel loved Earth and planned to journey back and forth many times. They discussed an exchange policy, where citizens from both Earth and Carthe could visit and learn the language and culture. Vel was told that they studied their genetic structure and discovered it is nearly identical to Earth people. They wondered if the genetic material was sprinkled throughout the Universe billions of years ago and that we all evolved similarly to become as we are now.

Vel stated that there is no reason to stop at what was accomplished here; we can send portals to other remote regions using robots, and set up links throughout the Universe. Of course that will take lots of time and money, but it can be done. We have given it a good start here. Vel climbed into the craft and sped home to Carthe. A little while later the craft came back with the robot and a note stating, "start your exchange at any time now."

ANGER MANAGEMENT

Bill Wright was just an average sized person. He was kind of a fearless guy for his size. When he was a teenager, he was coming home from a movie riding his bike. He wasn't feeling good and had a slight fever. As he reached the top of a hill, a known bully stopped him and challenged him to a fight. Bill got off his bike, and being tired and sick, he tried to talk him out of it. The bully sucker punched him and broke his nose.

Instant anger overcame Bill and he started for the bully. The bully looked at him in horror and ran off. Puzzled, Bill calmed down and went home. His father took him to the hospital to get his nose fixed, lecturing him all the way on the evils of fighting.

No one in his school ever challenged him again. The bully passed the word around that Bill was really a monster, not to be fooled with.

One day, after graduating from high school, Bill walked into the neighborhood store and was confronted by a gun wielding man that was trying to rob the place. The cashier/owner, an older woman, was pleading for mercy. The man grabbed her by the hair and was hurting her. Bill, to this point in his life, hardly ever lost his temper.

However, seeing this woman he's known for years, in pain, did the trick. He grabbed the gunman with one hand and threw him out of the front plate glass window. When the police arrived, the woman was babbling incoherently, saying that Bill had turned into a huge muscular hero and saved her life. The police looked at him and told him that he had won himself a friend for life. They laughed and patted him on the back.

Back home, he reflected on what had happened and tried to figure out how he was able to accomplish what he did. His deed made the newspapers and subsequently he was awarded a medal. His father stopped by and asked him if there was anything bothering him that he would like to talk about. Bill told him no, and thanked him for his concern.

A year later, Bill was driving his van down the major highway, when suddenly a car in front of him veered into another car causing a three car pile up. Bill pulled over and saw that two cars had a third car pinned upside down. The occupants of the two cars got out safely. The pinned car was smoking and leaking gas. The occupants were screaming and unable to get out. Bill became very angry at the driver who caused the accident, seeing that person run cowardly away. Bill ran down, flipped the cars off of the pinned car, ripped the doors off of it and pulled four shocked people to safety. Bill noticed the horror on the faces of all the witnesses. As the pinned car caught fire and exploded, he climbed into his van and drove away from the scene.

The next day, newspapers gave an account of a huge muscular being that rescued four people from certain death. Bill was very confused by the story; he did the rescue not a huge muscular being. When his father came to visit him for some recreational fishing; he told him he needed to talk. While fishing, he recounted to his father all the strange things that had happened to him since he was a kid. His father told him that he thought he knew what had been causing his problems. He asked him if these things happened when he got angry. Bill told him yes. He told Bill that before he said any more he would like them to visit a doctor friend of his in the city.

They drove to the city the next day and went into a professional building. They met with the doctor friend. His father conferred with the doctor privately and when they came back they asked Bill to let the doctor take a blood sample. He agreed and the doctor took the samples. Later the results of the tests were explained to Bill and his father. The doctor told them that it was as he suspected, Bill has the same genetic anomaly that you have. You both have an extra gene that other homo sapiens do not. He told Bill that he had kept his fathers condition secret for years. We were both in the Navy working in a secret area. He told him that while working with a top secret experiment, the material came loose exposing his father to harmful radiation. During the exposure his body grew all out of proportion and huge. He returned to normal quickly and had no apparent ill affects. The Navy kept this entire information secret. Years later, they declassified the information after which we tested your father and found the genetic anomaly. We discovered that when your father gets angry, the gene causes temporary abnormal growth and unbelievable strength. Fortunately your father is a very mild mannered man and believes that he has had no more than one or two occurrences in his lifetime. He told Bill that he must realize what has been happening to him and that he has inherited the same genetic anomaly from his father. He advised Bill to take a course in anger management.

He also told him that the secret he has kept for his father, he will keep for him.

The doctor told Bill that the changes to his body during anger probably went unnoticed by you but don't be shocked if you confront a mirror during the occurrence.

Later Bill took a course in anger management and kept his anger in check to the best of his ability. Still there are times when it's just beyond ones control. It did happen again and it involved Bill and his father. They went on a camping trip in the Canadian woods.

They picked a beautiful camp site next to a lake. The lake was teeming with fish and after finishing a breakfast of rainbow trout, they decided to explore the area. They pushed their way through a heavily wooded area and started up the side of a mountain. They were very high up; the view below stretched for miles into a lush green valley. Having decided to go back, they reached the edge of the woods. Their way was blocked by an angry grizzly bear. The bear swiped Bill and knocked him down. Bill looked up to see a huge being grab the bear and toss him several feet away. As the bear ran off, scared stiff, Bill saw the huge being turn into his father. As his father helped him up, Bill asked if that was what he turned into when he got angry? He told him that it was probably similar.

They went back to the camp site and continued to take advantage of the great fishing. They were enjoying their fish lunch when they noticed two or three bears watching from the edge of the woods. Bills father picked up a string of fish, walked toward the bears, and tossed the fish at them. They snatched it up and disappeared into the woods.

Days later, when they decided to return home, they packed up all their equipment and started back to the area where their car was parked. Upon reaching the area, they were surprised by a pack of hungry wolves. They started at Bills father; Bill lunged forward, grabbed the wolf and disabled him. Spontaneously, the wolves were all over them. Suddenly the wolves stopped their attack and ran off. Bill and his father were surprised until they saw the reason; the bears had come to their rescue. They had made some friends on the trip that they never expected.

AN AGENTS EYES

Paul Dowd had been an FBI Agent for 25 years and lived with his wife all that time in Colorado. His job took him all over the country on many dangerous assignments. His skills and ability were second to none. He received many awards and was considered the best in the field. His wife Rose was very proud and devoted to him.

They had no children but were happy with their status.

While browsing through secret files on his computer he uncovered a plot to kill the Attorney General of the United States. It appeared to be masterminded by someone in the Bureau. Codes that he acquired over the years gleaned this information for him. Although not revealing the mastermind, he was able to determine when and where it was planned to be executed. Not knowing who to trust he rushed to the scene.

Thrusting himself between the assassin and the Attorney General and was killed, the assassin was killed by other agents. His heroic efforts were rewarded posthumously and received by his grieving wife. He was buried at Arlington National Cemetery. As dictated in his will, his body parts were donated where needed. His eyes were donated to a young man who had been blind for many years. His eyes were destroyed by an accidental acid spill when he was ten years old. The young man's name is Peter Evens.

Despite his blindness, Peter kept himself in great shape and excelled in swimming, weight lifting, wrestling and

Karate which awarded him a Black Belt.

After the surgery, he felt a strange presence in his head he could not understand. When the Doctors removed the bandages and he saw the light of day for the first time in 15 years the presence identified himself. The voice of Paul Dowd, through thought, told Peter that he didn't know how but he was seeing also. He told Peter that he could share his thoughts and sight but had no other control. He told Peter that at first he was horrified by what happened but then realized it had happened for a reason. He explained what happened to him and who he had been before being killed. After a detailed explanation of what was going on he finally convinced Peter to join him in a concerted effort to right a wrong and bring a traitor to justice.

Peter started by applying to the FBI for a job. With Paul's help he aced the entrance exam and was inducted for training. He had the same success with the training and graduated at the top of his class. At the graduation ceremony Paul noticed his widow Rose in the crowd. He talked Peter into approaching her and introduced himself as a friend of her late husband. She was immediately captivated by his eyes and after gazing more closely passed out cold. When she came to, she apologized and stated that she thought she was looking at her dead husband. Paul decided that was a bad decision and they agreed to leave her alone.

Now in a position to pursue the traitor, Peter with Paul's secret codes and access, uncovered the plot to kill the Attorney General and the identity of the mastermind.

To his surprise, the culprit is his immediate supervisor. Paul advised Peter to be very careful. This man is very clever and might already suspect him. The next day Peter is sent out on a very dangerous assignment. He was sent to investigate a Warehouse. When he arrived, he was confronted by assassins, but he was ready with Paul's help and took out two of them and captured a third.

With persuasive methods learned from Paul he got the

assassin to tell all. With testimony, the whole plot is revealed. Before he could be brought to trial the traitor committed suicide. Peter was awarded a Medal, and a promotion to supervisor. In the coming years Peter is decorated many times and eventually promoted to a top position.

Paul, having accomplished his objective slowly recedes into the depths of the subconscious of Peter's brain. There he will remain unless needed again.

THE TEMPLE

The temple was a huge stone edifice located in Beijing, China. It had a large arching doorway and stone steps leading in. The outside was dark red with gold markings with some kind of coded message carved intricately in stone. Visitors could walk through the temple during the day, but needed to get out before nightfall. Many people have gone in, stayed too long and disappeared.

A visiting American and his grandson walked by close to evening, and got startled by all the people running out. When he was told the tale and why they ran out, he laughed. The next day they decided to spend the afternoon exploring the temple.

They were amazed at the construction of huge marble stones with intricate carvings.

They passed statues and tablets related to the many dynasties of China's past. They remarked at how closed it felt for a complete open structure. The view from all sides was lofty; one could see for miles in all directions. The structure was long; it took all afternoon to complete the tour. Visitors were leaving toward dusk, so they decided to leave also. Going down the stone steps, the grandson mentioned that he had forgotten his hat and ran back to get it. He was gone quite a while as it got dark. The American had no choice; he had to return for his grandson. People watching him go in gasped and hollered at him not to go in

The American, Professor Adams, was a history teacher

at Harvard University, in Cambridge, Massachusetts. He scoffed at the people hollering at him and went in. Once inside everything looked different from his earlier visit. He hesitated and started back but the exit was no longer there. The ceiling was still open but the sides were much higher and there was no outside view. There was a strange eerie light about the place; he had no trouble seeing. Where there were just statues before, there were now archways alongside each statue. A trip around the temple went a lot faster than earlier, but he saw no sign of his grandson. Completely puzzled, he decided to wait until morning to get out. Morning never came; he was stuck there in time.

ARCHWAY #1-ZHOU

Having taught Chinese history at Harvard, he thought the best place to look for his grandson would be through one of the archways. He chose the early dynasty. His knowledge of past Chinese history and language skills would help him. He understood the works of the early kings in the Zhou dynasty. He walked through the opening and came out into the country side. He looked to go back but saw no opening that he just came through. The temple was there in the same location. Nothing else was the same. He talked to workers in the fields and determined he was at King Wen's time.

King Wu, the son of King Wen, was in power. Prof. Adams had arrived at a time when King Wu was contemplating an attack on the Shang. The Prof. could not believe this was happening to him. He gathered himself together and accepted his situation. Seeing past history in the making was beyond his wildest dreams. He was arrested by palace guards and brought before King Wu. The king was about to order this strangers execution, thinking him a spy of the Shang king, Zhouxin, but changed his mind when the

Prof. informed the king that he was sent by the gods and was heaven's representative on earth. He proceeded to tell the king that heaven was with him and would ensure his victory over the Shang with proper council from heaven's representative. Prof. told the king to attack the Shang now; they are at their weakest and victory is assured. Not daring to do otherwise in case he was heaven's representative, the king had his warriors attack. The advice worked, the attack was a complete success. The Shang king committed suicide in disgrace. The king was convinced that the Prof. was sent by the gods and appointed him as advisor to the king.

He was treated royally and given land, wealth and respect. In his position, he was able to look for his grandson at will. He could not find him but found a few others that had been trapped as he was. Three years later, King Wu died, leaving control to his brother, the duke of Zhou. The duke never favored Prof. Adams. Fearing for his life, the Prof. rounded up the others, gathered all his wealth and entered the temple in the evening. He was trapped as before. He had convinced the others that with him they had a chance of getting back home. Back in the temple, he was as before, no time had passed. That was the same for the others with him. He began to understand what was happening.

ARCHWAY # 2– SONG

The Prof. urged by his love of history decided to go along with this puzzle. He entered the archway into the Song dynasty with his loyal followers.

They had become a cohesive team following the Prof. wherever he ventured. They were pretty badly treated in the last dynasty; some were even treated as slaves and prostitutes.

Professor Adams told his team that he recognized the period that they were in and that it was the Song dynasty year, 1004 AD. They had arrived during a peaceful period that lasted about 100 years. The Song army was defeated by the Liao and in humiliation agreed to make annual payments of 100,000 ounces of silver and 200,000 bolts of silk

The Prof. created a plan that would have them branch out in several areas looking for others in their situation as well as his grandson. Fortunately the Prof. had accumulated a fortune in silver and credentials while in the Zhou dynasty. Some of the team couldn't speak Chinese; they would have to double up with those that could. In any case he gave them enough silver that would speak for itself. They agreed to meet again in six months. It was the hope of the Prof. that anyone who entered a given archway in the temple would come out into the exact same time period making any search for people more feasible.

He headed to the palace of the Emperor Taizong. He was stopped by Palace guards and convinced them that the Emperor would want to talk to him. The Emperor was amazed at his story and offered him protection while in the Beijing area. He spent months looking for his grandson and others and came up with nothing. After six months he went back to the agreed meeting place. His team was all there with several other people that were in the same situation as them. They all agreed to follow the Prof. as their leader. The new people were from all over, some from China, Britain, Germany, France and Spain. Some were soldiers, nurses, doctors and engineers.

They went back to the temple, entered during the night time, and looked for another archway. Professor Adams made it clear to all that if they were to survive, they must work together with varied responsibilities. They entered the archway of the Mongol Yuan dynasty.

ARCHWAY #3-YUAN

The Prof. knew that the Mongol Yuan Dynasty was under the leadership of Kublai Khan and that his Empire stretched from Korea and Western Russia to Burma and Iraq. The Prof. sent his team to seek out the six Ministers that were charged with the responsibility to implement policy by Kublai Khan. From his team he would need experts in personnel, revenue, justice, public works and war. Their tasks would be to find the Minister that was responsible for each separate area and find a position of trust reporting to him. The Prof. would seek out scholars such as, Xu Heng, Yao Shu, and Wang E and help them with the writing of Chinese history. His plan was to get into a trusted position and gain wealth and status which would enable them to seek others that were trapped as they were and to gather them together.

Kublai Khan restored Chinese ideology of Confucianism and built temples and set up ancestral tablets in this period. The Prof. wondered if their temple originated at this time. His connection with the scholars proved successful and was instrumental in his finding his grandson. His grandson was busy helping with Chinese history. Their reunion was joyful in spite of the circumstances. The Prof. filled him in on what was happening and told him that they would be leaving soon.

As agreed, the team met again at a designated place. Several additional people were added to the team. Most of them had stories of success but some failed and would not be going back with them. One woman had a heart attack and died.

The names of these people were recorded for their relatives when and if they got back.

One team member had a story she heard from an old priest that a Wizard in the Shang dynasty put a curse on a temple after the defeat of the Zhou. King Wu had the Wizard tortured and dismembered. According to the priest, the curse could be removed but only by a descendant of the Wizard. The Prof's grandson said that he remembered

something about that in the historical records he was studying. He remembered that a coded phrase must be read by a
descendant. They all returned to the temple at nightfall.
Again the Prof. told his team the importance of working together. The new members pledged their support. Back in
the temple, there were many additional members; who all
voiced their support of the Prof's leadership. With renewed
resolve and the intent to gather more trapped people, they
entered the archway to the Ming dynasty.

ARCHWAY # 4- MING

Outside the temple and in the Ming dynasty, the Prof.
pulled the team together for a strategy meeting. He told
them that there were over fifty of them now and that they
needed to reorganize. He asked all French speaking, Spanish speaking, etc. to group together. He counted four groups.
He told them to select a leader and record the names in
each group. That done, he asked for anyone that could
speak Chinese and a language in any of the groups to step
forward. Four people stepped forward. He asked each one
to join a group as interpreter. He then asked for any person
that has skills in breaking codes to step forward. One person who was bilingual in Chinese and English stepped forward. The Prof. told him his task would be to break the
code on the front of the temple. He explained that it could
be what is needed to get us back. He told the others to look
for people in the same situation as us and anyone that has
information about the Wizard. He and his grandson would
research historical documents that they might find.

Also as part of every ones responsibility, they should
try to locate any possible descendants of the Wizard.

As before the Prof. knew where he was and its history.
The Ming dynasty lasted nearly three centuries, from 1368
to 1644. It existed between the Mongol Yuan dynasty and

the Manchu Qing dynasty. The founder of the Ming dynasty was Zhu Yuanzhang or Hongwu Emperor. The main social order was the educated elite and the uneducated masses.

To determine exactly what time period they were in, he had to learn what Emperor was in power and anything else that would give him a clue. He noticed that hundreds of ships were being built. This told him that the time frame was between 1405 and 1433. Also, he noticed that the capital was in Beijing. He remembered that Zhu's son Zhu Di, the Yongle Emperor, had moved the Capital in the year 1421.

Zhu Di's grandson Zhu Zhanji the fifth Ming Emperor led seven Maritime expeditions from 1405 to 1433. That would explain all the ships.

The Prof. directed the different groups to the four quadrants of the dynasty. He and his grandson would concentrate on Beijing. As agreed they would report in six months. In Beijing, they noticed a lot of new construction and they heard that construction was active on a Great Wall and that there were improvements to the Grand Canal linking Beijing with the Huang He and the Yangtze River. Six months passed very quickly and all the team members met again at the agreed to place. The reports by each group had some disappointing news and some good news. The group that went to the north got involved in the attacks by Zhu Di against the Mongols. Five of their group was killed and no new people were found.

The rest of them were lucky to get back. The group that went to the east had success in ship building, made many friends, and earned the respect of the elite because of their innovations and suggestions. They found twelve people that were in the same plight and that were happy to join the team.

The group that went south got involved in the Canal Linking project. They also had great success and came back with more people happy to join the team.

The group that went west got involved in the building of the Great Wall. They also were very successful and came back with many people happy to join the team.

The Prof. and his grandson had good news; they discovered the names of the Wizards descendants. They were able to recruit a few more people for the team.

Another piece of good news came from the person that was working to solve the code that was carved in the temple wall. He was able to solve the code in Chinese. Translated in English it was as follows:

"IF YOU BE MY DESCENDANT
PLACE BOTH HANDS ON THE
WRITING AND WISH THE CURSE
BE GONE BUT, BEWARE, IF YOU
BE NOT MY DESCENDANT YOU
WILL BECOME PART OF THE
WRITING"

The Prof. gathered the lists of new people and those deceased.

They all retreated into the temple at nightfall and were faced with the last Archway which led to the Qing Dynasty that was in power from 1644 to 1911.

Before entering, the Prof. dispersed the new members into their proper group. He advised the team that the number one task was to find a descendant of the Wizard. They entered and went all directions as they did before.

ARCHWAY # 5- QING

The Prof. knew that the Qing Dynasty was the last of the Chinese Dynasties and that Qing means "pure". He knew that a revolution would erupt in 1911 and that the boy

Emperor, Henry Pui would step down from the throne marking the end of the Qing Dynasty. To determine what date they had come into, they had to find out who was in power and what was happening.

The Prof. read a notice that Emperor Kangxi was holding a special examination to recruit scholars to document the history of the Ming Dynasty. This told the Prof. that the year was 1679.

The Prof. and his grandson were granted an audience with the Emperor. They were able to convince him of their expertise and knowledge and were recruited to help with the literary projects.

In their position of advantage, they were able to find several descendants of the Wizard. As the six month time period was coming close, they were able to convince one descendant to try and get rid of the curse. The convincing took a small fortune in silver.

At the six month period, they all gathered at the agreed to place. Very little of consequence was reported, except a few more people were added to the team. They confronted the temple and had the descendant place his hands on the writings.

He wished the curse be gone as told by the writing. Suddenly, a great flash of light blinded all of them. Then when they could see again, they saw the descendant imbedded in stone. He looked like part of the building but his face was distorted in an expression of horror; he was still holding the bag of silver. Evidently he was not a descendant of the wizard and went along for the silver.

Faced with this great set back, the Prof. told them not to lose faith and that there was nothing to be gained by going back into the temple. He told them that the answer has to be in this dynasty. The Prof. had them set up camp in their present area. He told that them there was food and water in the nearby village and that he was going back to the library in search of a real descendant of the wizard.

Back in the library, his research led him to a priest by the name of Chin, who lived nearby in Beijing. When he reached the home of Chin, he noticed many artifacts that reminded him of the temple. Chin was a very amiable man and welcomed the Prof. into his home. In the ensuing conversation, the Prof. related his story and the mystery of the temple. Chin said that he was definitely a descendant of the wizard and that he had many artifacts that were handed down from him. Chin knew of the tale of the curse and had decoded a message that was part of it, and was very surprised that the curse was real. He told the Prof. that he would do anything he could to help them.

When they arrived at the temple, all the people stood up and greeted Chin. Chin marveled at the building that his ancestor had cursed. He stepped forward placed his hands on the writing and uttered the message. Suddenly, the man stuck in the stone was released and fell to the ground. Beside him was a bag of silver. People appeared adding to the group, those that were killed also appeared and alive. Chin told them that if they all would enter the temple they will find their way back to their time. The man that was imbedded in the stone reached for the bag of silver, but the Prof. grabbed it and handed it to Chin saying, "he earned it and saved your life." He told Chin that he knew that he would use it wisely to help others. Chin handed the Prof. an amulet and told him that it would remind him of their visit. He shook his hand and thanked him for saving them and he entered the temple with all the others. Inside the temple they were confronted with archways back to their time, they all thanked the Prof. as they wished him goodbye. The Prof. and his grandson entered their archway and returned to the exact time that they had left. They looked back at the temple and his grandson told him he was going back for his hat The Prof. thought, oh no, but a minute later his grandson came out wearing his hat. As they walked along they noticed a statue that they hadn't seen before; it was of Chin, the plaque read "In memory of a great priest who helped many." The Prof. told his grandson that it looks like I picked a winner and asked where he would like to visit next. His grandson told him, home, home sweet home.

THE WIZARD

The year was 1679, the place Beijing China. The Emperor Kangxi was in power. A man by the name of Chin had just released a group of people from an ancient curse. The curse was put on by a Wizard, an ancestor of Chin's. Chin received a fortune in silver for his efforts and proceeded to help many poor people. His reputation became widespread and earned him the love and respect of many people. He had many relics that were left to him by his ancestors and while opening an old trunk again he noticed, for the first time, that it had a false bottom. When he investigated he found an old book. He opened the book and read as follows:

> In the 12th year of each century it will be necessary for a chosen person to operate a Great Lever which opens a door-way to the Universe. This doorway will release dark energy which will continue to overcome gravity and keep the Universe expanding. If this can't be accomplished, then the Universe will collapse ending all existence. The closing of this book will tell all.

Chin closed the book and found himself transported to a great room filled with some people that he recognized as his ancestors. A recent ancestor stepped forward and explained to him that everyone in this room was a Wizard and that they were all related to him. He further explained that they go back thousands of years and have been keeping the Universe expanding by operating a Great Lever. Once they have completed their task they no longer have the power to do it again. Only a chosen descendant can accomplish the task. They all hoped that the chosen one would be him. With that he took Chin to the Great Lever and asked him to turn it if he could. A tense moment occurred when at first it would not turn, and then it moved and finally opened the door all the way. The room full of past Wizards all cheered and his ancestor remarked that he was a chosen one. He was told that the energy will last for 100 years and then they would need another chosen one to keep it going.

Chin was told that he was now a Wizard with amazing powers that they would teach him how to use and control. He was told that it does have certain limitations; each spell will take a given amount of power, leaving your powers weaker until you release the spell returning your full power. His training continued for a long time, yet when he was returned to his home, he was right at the time that he had closed the book. Chin lived a highly respected life and continued to keep the Universe expanding by passing the book on to his descendants. A statue was erected in Beijing in his honor.

Over three centuries later, another descendant of the Wizards, Wu opened the book and found himself confronted with the same circumstances as his ancestors. He also was a chosen one and was able to turn the Great Lever keeping the Universe expanding. He was given all the necessary training and advised to keep a low profile in this century because jealous leaders would try to obtain his power. He was told the story of the Wizard who was tortured and finally dismembered by a jealous Emperor. Wu took all this advice very seriously; however certain circumstances led him to leave himself open to danger.

In the year 2012, Iran threatened global nuclear war by attacking Israel. Israel retaliated with nuclear weapons. Ultimately the whole mid east was sucked into the war with the US, UK and others being on alert as well. Only one country was holding out that Iran needed for support, China. While China was contemplating its course of action, Wu saw an opportunity to influence its decision. Wu went to the Chinese leader to show him what global nuclear war would do to the Earth. Wu demonstrated his power by showing the future devastation and the collapse of the Universe. Wu had to divulge too much to be convincing. He told the Chinese leader that the door to the Universe was located on Earth and that if certain people on Earth are destroyed so will the Universe. China stayed out of the conflict and everything settled down leaving only Iran to deal with. Wu realized that he was now in a very dangerous position. He cast a spell on his little one room house so that the inside was in another dimension and had many rooms and halls and his great throne- like- chair at the end of a very long hall. As Wu had suspected, one night soldiers of the Chinese leader came to the front door, forced their way in and were shocked at the size of the inside area. They composed themselves and began a search for Wu. They came to the very long hall and saw Wu sitting at the end. They pressed forward as Wu asked, "What do you want?" They said, "you're to come with us." Wu said, "Come and get me." They grabbed for Wu but he was not there; what they saw was just a specter. Shocked they backed off and ran as four large lions started after them. Later an army of men with many weapons came after Wu; however when they entered his home there was just the one room in the house and Wu was gone. The Chinese leader had his original soldiers executed for lying to him.

Wu decided to leave Beijing and travel to the Himalayas. He was granted an audience with the Dalai Lama and before he could explain his situation, the Dalai Lama said he knew why he was there and offered him sanctuary. Wu told him that he did not intend to stay long because he knew that if the Chinese leader found out it would make the Dalai Lama's relationship with China even worse. In the many meetings they had together Wu mentioned that the Earth has a doorway to the Universe which permits the release of dark energy that keeps the Universe from collapsing into a singularity ending all life. The Dalai Lama told Wu that he understood the critical nature of his mission in life was to protect the door and offered him fifty men for his use and protection. Wu told him that he would like to create a haven inside one of the mountains which he could accomplish with a powerful spell at his command. The Dalai Lama agreed, and watched as a beautiful marble edifice was carved into a mountain one thousand feet above the ground and spanning a gorge accessible by a 200 ft bridge. The edifice had fortifications for his fifty men and rooms for them and their families.

Meanwhile the Chinese leader became obsessed with finding Wu; he combed all areas in and around Beijing. After finding no sign of him, he expanded his search and then ultimately to the Himalayas. Spies told him that a great edifice existed inside of one of the mountains and nobody knew how it got there. The Chinese leader sent an emissary to the Dalai Lama demanding to know about any structure built inside of a mountain that may be sheltering a traitor.

The Dalai Lama wouldn't tell him anything which enraged the leader. He ordered his troops to invade the area and hold the Dalai Lama hostage. He sent ten troops across the bridge; they went inside but never came back. After that, they bombarded the side of the mountain destroying the bridge but otherwise causing little or no damage to the building. At that point the leader had two choices: 1. starve them out or 2. Drill a hole from the top of the mountain into the building and drop in a bomb. He decided on the second approach; he could always revert to the first if the second didn't work.

It took several days for his men to set up drilling equipment, which was brought in by helicopter. Once set up the drilling continued for several days until they finally reached inside the building. The timed bomb was dropped into the hole leaving plenty of time for the drillers to leave the mountain. Wu and his men huddled in an alcove away from the bomb. The explosion caused a big split in the mountain and sent the drilling equipment tumbling into the chasm below. Many of Wu's men were injured and needed aid; he was uninjured. Wu decided for the sake of his men that he would surrender if his men were given help. The leader agreed to the terms but left them trapped in the building as they whisked Wu away by helicopter. The leader had Wu brought back to Beijing and chained him in an underground dungeon. The leader accused him of being a traitor and told him that he would go easy on him if he would divulge the secret of his power. When Wu would not tell him, the torture began. Wu warned him and said, "If I die you will all die." Wu's power was very much diminished because of the spell he was holding to keep the mountain building intact for the protection of his men. Wu was growing very weak but refused to tell. In a goading statement made by his torturer, he was told that he was going to die just like all of his men that were killed in the mountain building. That's all Wu needed to hear; he immediately released the spell from the mountain in the Himalayas, regained his full power and disappeared right in front of the Chinese leader.

After having tried elaborate ways to elude the leader, he decided to try a simple approach. He disguised himself as a blind beggar and set himself in plain sight in Beijing square. It worked, nobody paid any attention to a blind beggar. He was known as Chan to other beggars and to other people that gave him charity, whom he will never forget. One day his sister was shopping and stopped by Chan to give him a few coins. She looked back abruptly, and said, "Wu is that you?" He said, "You must be mistaken lady my name is Chan." She walked away very puzzled. She came back each day, watching him with curiosity. Finally, she approached him and said, " I know it's you Wu, is this what your wizardry has brought you to?" He said, "Please Kim, don't let on that you know me; my life depends on it. I'll meet you tonight to explain. Let me know where you live and I'll be there around midnight." She told him and later that night they had their reunion. He explained as much as he could to her and she told him that his family missed him very much. She introduced him to her little son, Wong; he told her that their reunion would be very short because of the danger of the leader finding out that she was his sister. He told his sister to take good care of her son; he is a descendant of Wizards and could save the Universe some day. He gave her an amulet and told her to hold it in her hand and repeat his name three times and he will come to her. Wu went back to his corner in the square the next day and greeted his usual friends. This day he was greeted by an American who dropped money in his cup. Before the American could leave Wu asked him where he got that amulet. The American told him that he wouldn't believe him if he told him. Wu told him that he might if his name was Professor Adams. The Prof. stepped back and said, "That's a good guess for a blind man." Wu said, "yes I'm not blind but it was not a guess, your story and the Temple was handed down to me from my ancestor Chin." The Prof. said, "Well, it just happened to me and to your ancestor over 300 years ago if you can believe it." Wu said, "I believe it, your story and coming was foretold in folklore over the years; as a matter of fact the present Chinese leader's ancestor was one of the people released and he wouldn't be here today if it didn't happen." The Prof. asked him why he was disguised as a blind beggar. Wu related some of the things the leader was doing to him in an attempt to learn about his power.

The Prof. had become famous with the Chinese people because of his heroic involvement with the Temple. He offered to talk to the leader to see if he could get him to back off. Meanwhile the story of the Temple and Prof. Adams had just reached the Chinese leader. He was somewhat humbled by what he had heard and was happy to meet with the Prof.. The Prof. explained the importance of keeping Wu and his descendants free from harm. He explained that other nations may try to obtain the power, but it would result in disaster for all people in the Universe and it's China's responsibility to protect that power. He told the leader that Wu was a personal friend of his and that he would stand by and protect him to the best of his ability. He told him that the information about the Temple should be kept secret. After his talk, the leader realized the error of his ways and said that he would see that Wu and his descendants were protected. In the future the story will be considered a fantasy.

A GIANTS LEGACY

Herc sat back in his huge comfortable chair, stared into the crackling fire in the fireplace and then back at his grandchild and said, "say that again?" His grandson John, said, "grandfather, tell me about your father. What was he like? Where did he live? When did he die?" Herc looked at his grandson and said, "It's a long story but if you really want to know I'd have to start at the beginning." "It goes something like this."

My father, your namesake, John Hatcher, lived a long distance from here in a small town nestled in the White Mountains of New Hampshire. He loved to fish and ski and the mountains and the lakes offered him wonderful places to do both. He met your grandmother, Ann Phillips, at a lake on a boating trip. They spent a romantic summer together and decided to get married in the fall. The year was 1919, just after the 1st World War. Your great-grandfather was in the United States Army and went overseas to fight the Germans. He came back after the Germans were defeated with a hero's medal and a metal plate in his head from a German bomb. They got married in a small ceremony and afterward went on a motor trip to Canada. As they were driving along, they saw a bright object in the sky coming their way. They pulled over to the side of the road to watch it; they were fascinated and worried at the same time. He had seen incoming missiles before but nothing like that. The object came closer and closer and soon it lit up the whole visible sky. All of a sudden it crashed into the ground creating a huge hole and causing dirt and foliage to fly in every direction. The fiery mass was sparking and burning rapidly. John and Ann were visibly shaken but couldn't resist the temptation of getting a closer look at the object. They got out of the motor vehicle and approached the object; that action proved to be a bad mistake. The radiation from the object blistered their exposed body parts and turned their clothes to rags. They stumbled back to the motor vehicle and managed to drive to a nearby town and a doctor. The doctor told them that they got there just in time to prevent serious injury. Their honeymoon was a disaster but they recovered from their ordeal. They learned later that the object was a meteor. Herc stopped the story and said, "John, that's enough for now I've got to get up early tomorrow to go hunting."

The next day his sons gathered with Herc and went off hunting. A few hours later they stopped on top of a ridge and could see in the valley below a herd of caribou over a mile away. Herc grabbed his trusty rifle, aimed and pulled off four quick shots downing four caribou. The caribou weren't concerned about their felled companions until seconds later when they heard the shots, and then they bolted away. Herc said, "That should feed the family for a while; he told his sons to go get the meat and bring it to your wives," They responded, "Ok dad, do you want one for yourself?" Herc replied, "No bring them to your wives, they'll cut it up and distribute it."

That evening John came by with several of his sisters and brothers. John said, "Grandpa I've brought my sisters and brothers, they want to hear your story also." Herc replied, "Gee, you only brought twenty I'm glad you didn't bring them all. Are there more that might want to hear the story? If there are more, I'd like to tell this story just once, not several times. I'll call the family together. If they agree, we can do this in the big hall." It was agreed by the family, to have Herc tell his story to all interested. One of the family, a scribe, would record the story for posterity. The hall was packed with a number of Hercs children, spouses, grandchildren and friends. Herc repeated the story that he had told his grandson John and continued the story.

John and Ann went back to their apartment and set up housekeeping. Later Ann told John that she was pregnant. She went to a doctor for a checkup; the doctor told her that everything was coming along fine for her being six months along. Ann told the doctor that was impossible and that she just got pregnant a month ago. The doctor told her that she must be mistaken and that there's a fairly well developed fetus in her womb. A month later her water broke and she was rushed to the hospital because of severe pain and an inability to deliver the baby. The doctor told her the baby was huge and that he would have to operate to deliver the baby. The baby was delivered weighing sixteen pounds. The doctor said the baby is healthy and as strong as Hercules. The name stuck, they shortened it to Herc.

Herc told the audience, "By now you must realize that the baby was me. My mother got well quickly after the operation and marveled at my phenomenal growth. She took me back to the doctor who was also amazed at my growth. He did a test of my thyroid gland and determined that it was abnormal, contributing to the rabid growth. My father was sure that it was caused by the radiation we received from the meteor."

"My father was a Caucasian like me and was kind of short, only six feet tall. My mother was even shorter. My father was a carpenter and my mother a housewife. Before my sixth birthday both of them were killed in a house fire. As the flames from the fire were engulfing the second story of the building where we lived, they pushed me out of a window; I landed on my spring like feet, no problem, however they didn't make it; I still feel the pain of my losing them. I believe they are both angels in heaven waiting for me. After the death of my parents I was transferred to an orphan's home. I had a problem getting adopted by anybody because of my size. By the time I was ten years old I was almost six feet tall. Special desks and chairs had to be provided for me. I was ridiculed by my classmates because of my size and awkwardness from trying to adapt to small people's things. I tried out for sports but was rejected because it was considered unfair for the rest of the children. When I turned fourteen I had reached seven feet in height. I did not fit anywhere; too big for sports and furniture and most buildings and homes.

At that time, a couple adopted me, telling the agency that they really loved me and would make a nice home for me. When they got me to their home, everything changed; they didn't want a son, they wanted a slave. They had a secret gold mine and needed a strong person to help them with the excavation. They worked me ten to twelve hours a day and when I started to protest they chained me up. By the time I was sixteen I was eight feet tall and very strong from all the hard work. One day when I tried to rest, he brought a whip and laid a couple on me. I went kind of crazy; I broke my chains, picked him up and threw him several feet. He called the police and preferred charges against me. They didn't believe any of my wild stories. I was given two years in prison as an adult.

In prison I got my first experience with men of no morals; they didn't dare mess with me but I saw what they did to weaker people and I was completely disgusted. Being unable to do anything about it, I turned my efforts into learning a new trade. I learned to operate machinery, the bigger the better. I learned enough to design a rifle that would be made just for me. It would be longer than any existing rifle and very heavy, more like a cannon with repeater capability. I showed the plans to the Warden; he laughed and said to go ahead and build it, if that will keep me out of trouble. Before I finished my two year sentence, I had it completed plus a mold to make ammunition for the rifle. The Warden allowed me to keep the rifle in exchange for the money that I had earned in prison.

At eighteen years old, I was eight and a half feet tall and weighed four hundred pounds. I walked down Main St. in the town and noticed people looking at me in amazement and some ridiculing me as they went by. One woman crashed her vehicle into a building distracted by my presence. She blamed me for the accident and wanted me locked up. The judge dismissed the case but advised me to make myself scarce. I decided that I didn't belong in this civilization, I didn't fit anywhere with these little people. I went to my parent's lawyer to obtain the inheritance my parents left for me when I reached eighteen years of age. I received a check for one thousand dollars. I bought a train ticket to Canada and traveled as far the train would take me into Canada. I stayed in the town to buy powder, lead for my rifle, tools, shoes and warm clothing. I also had a blacksmith make me a long heavy knife that fit me perfectly. I met the first friendly people in my life in this town. The man was a Frenchman named Louis Derocher; Louis was a large man about seven feet tall. He worked as a lumberjack for a big logging company. He lived there with his sister, Marie. Herc said to the audience, "Yes she is Grandmother and Matriarch of you all. Let me continue. She was a large woman and wise and gentle in her ways. I got along very well with both of them. Louis told me that he never met anyone bigger than me. We shared some of his home made wine and after I beat him three times arm wrestling he gave up. When I told them it was time for me to leave they were very disappointed. They agreed to have supplies for me once a year at their place. I bought a pack mule and headed for the deep forest.

Finally, I reached my destination, right here where I live today. I don't have to tell you why I decided to settle here, the beautiful lake teeming with salmon and graylings.

The abundance of wildlife, caribou, wolves, moose, sheep, lynx, grizzlies and numerous other animals, a hunters dream come true. I built my first cabin, it had to be huge; the ceilings had to be twelve feet high and the doors eleven feet high. When I finished building it, I felt that I was finally home.

When I reached twenty-one years of age, I finally stopped growing. I was about nine feet tall and weighed about four hundred and fifty pounds. Later I attached a shed to the cabin for storage and I built a barn for livestock. One day as I was sitting in my big chair in front of the cabin, a grizzly bear approached me growling and threatening. It probably wanted to scare me into leaving the territory. I stood up my full nine feet and growled right back. The bear was stunned and sat down with a grunt seemingly bewildered. I went into the shed and came out with a big piece of meat. I handed it to the bear; he grabbed it and ran off. About a week later she came back with three cubs. I gave them more meat and we all became good friends. I played with the cubs while mother bear enjoyed eating some meat. They came back many times that season but as winter approached they didn't show at all. At that point the meeting was interrupted by loud banging against the outer fence. Herc dismissed the meeting and said they would resume at a later date.

Hercs sons were poised and ready to attack the bears that were banging on the fence; Herc told his sons to stand down. Herc recognized the bears as old friends; he opened the gates and let them in. They surrounded Herc and hugged him with joy. Herc ordered that all bears were to be fed. The bears were allowed to stay in the compound and let out in the morning. Herc called a meeting and told all, that the bears are our friends and they are to be treated as friends. They were fed by my orders and I take full responsibility for the food shortage. I'm calling for volunteers for a big hunt tomorrow." The next day the turn out was a little disappointing but enough showed to get the job done. They split up into teams, one hunter in each group and two or three runners to pick up the downed game. Because of the shortage of hunters, Herc was forced to go. They didn't go too far before they spotted a big buck deer about a quarter of a mile away. Easy for Herc, he downed it with one shot. They all proceeded to the kill; when they got there it was surrounded by wolves. Not willing to relinquish the kill, the wolves attacked the group. Herc was too close to use his rifle so he pulled out his knife and started slashing through the wolves. Eventually the wolves ran off but Herc was badly hurt. The group returned to the compound; Herc was brought to his cabin to be attended by his wife. The injury took a lot out of him; he spent a lot of time in bed and slowly got back on his feet but he was not as good as before. During his convalesance all his sons, their wives, and his grandchildren visited him. Finally he was able to resume his story and after much prodding by his family he got the group together in the big hall to hear his story.

Herc told the audience, "People, I'm not feeling the greatest but I will try to finish my story. The scribe told me where I left off. After years of hunting, I learned a lot about the woods. I knew that the bears hibernated every winter in a deep underground cave. During the winter of one year, I decided to explore the cave where the bears were sleeping. I saw the bears' lair and went by hoping not to disturb them. They knew who I was by my scent and weren't disturbed. I followed down into the cave using torchlight and ran into a wall of pure gold. I couldn't believe my eyes but having a bit of experience with gold mines, as I told you, I know gold when I see it. Using my knife I took a big chunk and put it in my knapsack. Back at my cabin, I took out my kit and gave the gold the acid test. It proved to be high grade ore. I started mining the gold and continued all winter long. I stripped the wall clean of gold; however there was plenty left throughout the cave. I stashed the many bags of gold in a secret hiding place and took enough back to the cabin to do what I had in mind. At winters end, I traveled to Louis and Marie for supplies. That year we couldn't hold back any more. Marie and I confessed our love for each other and at her request we got married in the Catholic Church in the village. Marie agreed to come and live with me wherever I go. I got Louis aside and told him that I had a place for him but I needed him to take care of one thing first. I gave him the exact map location of the lake and the thousands of acres surrounding it. I told him to go to the Capitol and buy the lake and all the land." Louis said, "Sure, with what my good looks?" I gave him a bag of gold. Then I told him that there was more where that came from and you will share in it. He was astonished and said he would take care of it. We agreed to meet next year at the compound. The next year he showed up with all the documents and I showed him another surprise that Marie and I had for him, a strapping son, and his nephew. I showed Louis the mine and told him he could take as much gold as he wanted.

After about a year, Louis got tired off digging for gold; he had so much he didn't know what to do with it. I showed him a master plan for the building of this waterfront area into a resort of our own. He loved it and wanted to start right away; I said all right but Marie is having another baby, it will have to wait a few days. Marie ultimately gave me eight sons and four daughters. As you all know they inherited my huge size. And all you grandchildren have got it too. Many of you have made me proud by traveling to universities and obtaining degrees. What is this game called basketball that universities are willing to give free tuition if you will play? Things sure have changed; now they want giant people. We even have aircraft pilots in the family. It sure saves us a lot of trouble when supplies are brought in by aircraft that can land right on the lake at our front door. I do not plan on dying right now but when I do I want John, my grandson, to have my rifle and knife. I hope they will be as good to you as they were to me. That's enough of the story; I hope your scribe got it all because I'm all done talking."

Herc finished his story, updating his life to the present time; however he left a few things out, as most autobiographers do. Back when Louis went off to the capitol to obtain a deed to the lake and property; he did a little celebrating. He exchanged the gold for Canadian money and opened bank accounts as Herc instructed, but after he obtained the deed; he did some drinking and bragging. The women loved it but unfortunately, so did some unscrupulous men that were watching him with interest. The men did some partying with him and heard enough that led them to believe that he had struck it rich. Louis got back with the deed all right but his new friends were not far behind.

They showed up a few weeks later after Louis arrived and they told him that they wanted part of the action. When Louis introduced them to Herc they were a little put off by his awesome size and told Herc that their weapons were equalizers. Sitting across from them, Herc told them that the blade at his side would lop off their heads the second they reached for their weapons. A tense moment was broken by Herc who told them not to act hasty. He offered a proposal that they could work the mine and keep the gold they collected less 30% that they would give to him. The men countered with a proposal of 20% which was finally agreed at 25%. Herc told them that they would need tools, food and shelter which he could provide at a cost, which they must pay before they started. The men paid the cost, collected the tools and were shown to the mine. The men came back once a week without any gold, claiming that they didn't have any luck. As winter came on, they didn't come back at all. Herc told Louis that they must have taken a lot of gold and taken off. When the weather cleared, Herc and Louis went to the mine to check things out. They discovered the bodies of the men; they were badly mutilated and bags of gold were stacked all around. Herc told Louis that the bears didn't like being disturbed by them and quieted them down, permanently. After that, Louis decided to leave the lake area and travel around the world. He took a fair amount of gold that he would need for the trip. Herc and Marie wished him luck and told him to come back when he got it out of his system. They missed him very much; he never came back. Herc gathered his family and told them that they were planning to build a huge complex around Bear Lake, with the addition of an airport, police station, schools and shops. We are planning to do all this and still provide a vast area of conservation. Also any area built and owned by us will provide sanctuary for bears. Marie and I will be going on a world tour; we invite all those who are able to join us. When we get back we hope to be surprised by the planned development being completed.

Marie and Herc traveled back to their earlier homes; Herc was surprised by his outward greetings; most people asked if he had played basketball when he was young. They used their private plane for continental travel. Their son, Steve piloted the plane. After touring Canada and the USA, they boarded a yacht, also owned by them, and continued their tour abroad. After almost two years, Herc started feeling poorly and they decided to go home. When they got home they were delighted with the new Bear Lake resort complex. Their new home was huge and filled with all modern conveniences including, TV's, computers and gadgets that they had never seen before. They flew into the new airport and were very impressed. The whole place was a paradise and designed to attract people to the splendor of the northwest. Herc was particularly impressed by the cave tour. The whole cave was provided with lighting and ramped for safety when traveling into the cave.

Hercs health continued to fail and after a long illness he passed away. A strange thing happened during the funeral; mourners were startled by a bright light in the sky coming

towards them. It loomed larger as it approached and pan-
icked the mourners as it crashed in the resort square not far
from them. It created a huge hole in the ground and was
burning vigorously and sending sparks in every direction.
Marie warned people to stay away from the object; it's
probably similar to the one that harmed Hercs parents. She
thought a while and then remarked; Herc came in with a
meteor and has gone out with one. They all wondered if it
was really a coincidence. Later a huge statue was erected in
the square, built on top of the meteor; it depicted Herc surrounded by his friendly bears.

A PLACE IN THE UNIVERSE

CHAPTER 1
DISCOVERY

Al and his wife Beth were amateur explorers; Al was a Physics professor and Beth an Archaeologist. They both took time off from work to explore the Mayans in the Yucatan of South America. Beth had researched the Mayan past civilization and had formulated a theory that there had to be a missing temple that was built by and for visiting aliens from outer space. She was convinced that the temple had to be located in an area that she had plotted by coordinates. They traveled to the Yucatan and discovered that the area that she had designated was extremely dense forest. Al said, "I can't believe anybody would build a temple in this jungle." Beth replied, "That's why nobody has discovered it yet." Her confidence inspired Al to go on. They hacked their way through dense jungle for many days enduring mosquitoes, snakes and unbelievable heat. Each night they had to clear an area to rest and build a fire for cooking. The nets helped to keep the mosquitoes away from them but the snakes were something else. They were nearly at the end of their endurance and concerned about their remaining water and food supply when Al thought he saw the outline of a building surrounded by the jungle. They hacked their way toward it and ultimately came upon a hidden temple. Their excitement almost overcame them as they plodded ahead unmindful of the great effort they were expending. Exhausted but elated they came to a wall in the temple that had all the signs of containing a doorway into it. Beth saw a possible doorway and had Al run his knife around the blocks to loosen up the door. They both pushed as hard as they could against that area of the wall and the door slowly moved.

Once in and with the aid of flashlights, they climbed up a winding and very cramped stone stairway. The stairway led up to a huge chamber where they found to their amazement, a console and a wall of solid glass-like material. At the console, they discovered two alien bodies dressed in rotted robes. The glass-like wall measured about 50ft.x50ft. Above them, the ceiling seemed to be split in the middle and hinged so that it could open up. Beth had studied the Mayan ancient language and was able to decipher the documents lying about and realized they had discovered the missing information that historians thought was destroyed by the Spanish. The documentation confirmed that the Mayans learned mathematics and astronomy from the aliens. This explained how they could have been so primitive in agriculture and tool making and yet so advanced in technology. Alien manuals described the operation of the wall and ceiling from the console and labeled the equipment as a direct doorway to their home planet. They carefully removed the two bodies from the console and sat down to check its operation. Its energy source that was from some unknown technology, seemed to be adequate, but they could not get it to operate. The alien manual mentioned a key but it was not in the console. Al noticed that the dead aliens had amulets around their necks. He placed them on Beth and himself and the console fired up; he had found the missing key. The glass like wall brightened up like a TV screen. Al walked over to the screen and was able to put his hand right through. He said to Beth, "This is the doorway to the alien planet; one of us could go through while the other stays behind to operate the console." Beth said, "It's very risky but we've come this far, let's go the rest." Without another word, Al entered, and a minute later came back and said, "It works; I was on the planet in a building with a huge laboratory and equipment just like we have here."

CHAPTER 2
THE ALIEN PLANET

Al said to Beth, "We were lucky the equipment on the planet was left on enabling us to connect and travel through. There wasn't anyone around; I looked down from the building and saw a major city completely void of people. The environment and climate is very much like that on earth." Beth said, "It appears that some major catastrophe struck and killed all life on the planet. From the documentation left here in the temple, the aliens were desperate and were trying to save their race. They tried to combine their DNA with the Mayans but were unsuccessful. It appears that the aliens had become so dependent on having everything done for them with robots and the like that they degenerated over the millenniums and could no longer propagate. They taught the Mayans math, astronomy and their language thinking to integrate them into their civilization. Too late the aliens tried other experiments with humans around the world but were also unsuccessful. They began to die and even crashed a spaceship in the United States. Their last hope was to keep this console open for return to their planet." Al said, "There is no reason why we both can't go together to the planet now, we can leave the equipment on and travel back and forth at will." They entered the doorway together and started exploring the planet and its great cities and technology they have inherited. Al found the technology fantastic and started reactivating systems that had been dormant for some time. Al discovered that in the main building they first arrived at from earth was the central control of all robotics on the planet. He changed their software to accept the English language and to respond to humans. They both agreed that trying to make this planet friendly to humans was too big a job for just the two of them. They decided to go back and study a way to bring help on board. Al learned the operation of one of the alien spacecrafts and took it for a test flight. He said to Beth, "This craft practically flies itself, I changed the computer software to respond to me and I believe we can fly this back to earth through the doorway." He and Beth did just that and traveled back to the temple. The doorway had ample room for the craft; obviously the aliens designed it for that purpose. They decided to fly the craft back home. Their estate in western Massachusetts was isolated enough for them to arrive reasonably undetected and the craft would fit easily into their garage. Using a remote alien device, Al opened the ceiling access and flew the craft up and out of the temple. The ceiling closed automatically and it was necessary to keep the console activated for return. During the trip back at incredible speeds many people from Mexico to the United States reported seeing a UFO.

CHAPTER 3
GATHERING HELP

Al and Beth parked the craft in their garage and went into the house. After a good nights sleep, they sat down to some serious discussion pertaining to gathering help.

They knew there was a credibility problem and had to select people that they thought could be trusted. They discussed seeking people from the following professions: computer engineering, agriculture, industry, law enforcement, government and social services. They called people they knew in each field and arranged to have them meet at their home for cocktails and dinner. They enjoyed their meeting and after dinner they sat down in the living room for coffee. Beth addressed the group and said, "ladies and gentlemen you are probably aware that we called you together for a reason. You all know that Al and I have been exploring in the Yucatan for a missing temple; well we found it." One person said, "your kidding, if you did why didn't you claim it in the Yucatan and how did you get back here so fast?" Beth replied, "That's what Al and I are about to disclose to all of you." They told the group of their trek through the jungle and their discovery of the temple. Then Al said, "When we entered the temple we found dead aliens sitting at a console that operated a door to a far distant galaxy." Another person said, "Come on, you don't expect us to believe that do you?" Beth said, "We know that what we have told you is hard to believe but everything we have told you is true and we can prove it. Did you notice in the news, that UFO's were reported as being sighted?

Well that was us flying from the Yucatan to here." The group were stunned at what they were hearing and started to get up to leave. Al and Beth directed them into the garage and pointed to the alien craft. They were all flabbergasted and intrigued at what they saw. Al said, "Jump in ladies and gentlemen were going to spend the next hour in the Yucatan." They all got in and in a few seconds they were airborne and traveling to the Yucatan at incredible speed. The group was speechless and astonished when they approached the temple and glided softly to the inside of the temple and watched the ceiling close automatically. Al said, jokingly. "There will be UFO reports this evening." The group apologized for not believing them and was excited to learn more. Al and Beth sat at the console and activated the screen. Al said, "You see before you the doorway to a distant Galaxy and the former home of the aliens; come with Beth and I and we will travel to the planet" They all held hands and entered together. They arrived at the building with the breathless group and were astounded by what they saw, but so were Al and Beth. They looked out into the city and observed many robots going about and performing a cleanup of the city; many dead alien bodies were brought to a crematorium for disposal. The signs had all changed to English and welcome signs were everywhere. A robot approached Al and Beth and said, "Sir and madam, we are at your command and recognize you as the true leaders of this planet. All has been arranged for your pleasure." Al said, "All of this has happened because I reprogrammed the central computer?" The robot said, "Yes sir; my name is Regal and all robots in the planet report to me. I report to you two." Al said, "I have to return to Earth now but I'll be back in a short while to hear your report." Regal told AL and Beth to take a robot with them; he will be needed to control the doorway for your exit and arrival and he will operate the equipment that conceals the temple and creates a force field around it protecting it from damage. Al and

Beth gathered the group and they returned to the temple. Beth told the group, "We will be leaving you at our house so that you can pick up your cars. We urge you to keep everything you've seen secret. You know what could happen if this information got into the wrong hands. Any of you that are ready to come with us now are welcome otherwise we will return in a week to pick up the rest of you. We leave you access to our home and hope to see you in a week." The computer engineer elected to come along with Al and Beth because he was single and he thought nobody would miss him. The rest of them needed time to make excuses so that their families would not be alarmed.

CHAPTER 4
A PLACE IN NEED

Al and Beth went right back to the temple: the robot saw in advance their coming and opened the ceiling door and guided the craft right into the temple. The robot welcomed them and asked permission to keep the craft for its use in case of an emergency. Al and Beth agreed and walked through the doorway to the planet and central control. They were immediately greeted by Regal and shown to a large conference room where they were seated at the head of a large long table. Regal was asked for a report and he was told that, "All was well now that you are here. The planet had been pretty well shut down since the former rulers' demise. The farms are back in operation and should be yielding crop in about 2 months; an agricultural person is needed to head up research. Industry is back up and running, robot repair and building needs a computer engineer to head the operation. Many human persons are needed in many areas; a complete list will be available soon." Al said, "We have your computer engineer right here; he is prepared to start now if you will show him his office. You are dismissed for now, this meeting is concluded." During the week, Beth and Al studied at the cities vast library and found out that this planet was in a dwarf galaxy formed in the early creation of the universe. The planet was located in a solar system in the outer perimeter of the galaxy. The galaxy has a small black hole in its center and has been evolving for billions of years. The planets projected life is less than one billion years. The planet has been around a lot longer than Earth and has advanced its technology far beyond Earth's. Al and

Beth agreed that many schools will be needed to bring our people up to date. They pulled together all the material they would need, plus the list of required skills. They told Regal that they would be back soon and were leaving their computer engineer in charge until they got back. They went into the temple and took the craft back to their home. When they got there everyone was waiting for them except the law enforcement person who left a message that he couldn't get away. Al and Beth went over all the reports and material that they brought back with the four remaining persons. They were all excited that they would be needed. They decided to sleep over and leave in the morning. In the middle of the night they were awakened by a loud amplified voice telling them to come out with their hands up in the air. Al said, "It looks like our law enforcement buddy has spilled the beans. What a fool; he could have had a trusted position in the planet. Don't worry people, once we get into the craft they can't hurt us." They loaded into the craft and zoomed out under a hail of bullets that had no affect on the craft. Beth said, well, there goes our beautiful estate; we will not be able to go back there again." When they got back to the temple the robot told them that it had to cloak the temple because many soldiers were trying to locate it as if they knew it was there somewhere. Al said, " good job, don't let them find it." They went into the doorway and into central command. Regal said that he knew the problem we were having with the temple and that we did not have to worry. The report from the computer engineer was more distressing; he said that he came upon information that Earth was going to be bombarded by several huge meteors in the year 2012 and there would be no way of avoiding it. The result would be a dust cloud around the planet that could last for 100 years. All living things would be affected and eventually die out similar to the great demise of the dinosaurs. They looked at each other and said, "We've got a place for everybody on Earth right here."

CHAPTER 5
THE EXODUS

They sat down in the conference room and tried to figure out a way to convince the people of Earth that they had a severe problem and needed to leave in a great exodus to avoid disaster. They decided to start with the United States and would contact the president through a close person to the president that they knew personally. This close person to the president lived in upstate New York in a remote area. Without giving her any warning they flew the craft right onto her estate and faced her with the evidence. She was shocked, but invited them in to discuss the situation. When they got finished they took her for a ride to the temple which thoroughly convinced her of immediate action. Later she approached the president and told her of her encounter. The president having known and trusted her for years believed her story and consented to a secret meeting with Al and Beth and her cabinet. After a trip to the temple and then on to the planet the president and cabinet had to agree that a mass exodus was necessary. The problem was now in the hands of the president; her task would be to convince the nation and the people of Earth that it would be necessary to evacuate. It took over a year, but after a lot of political infighting, she was able to convince many nations of the emergency and the plan to evacuate. The revelation of the temple and the planet was earth shattering for a lot of people; some leaders were never convinced and elected to stay to the detriment of their people.

Al and Beth decided to set up a doorway system in key

major countries to help expedite the exodus. Inhabitants watched with amazement while robots assembled the systems in their countries. As the units were completed people started leaving immediately. Taliban leaders watched as thousands of Arab people were leaving. Then they stopped all exiting and told the people that, "leaving is against our religious beliefs and that the story of the world ending is a fraud." When people continued to leave, they attacked the robots and tried to destroy the doorway system. Conventional weapons did not work so they used an atomic bomb that destroyed the robots, the doorway system and many of their people. Al and Beth had no choice but to leave millions of them to their fate. Unfortunately, the Taliban released terrorists to destroy the systems in all Arab countries using atomic weapons and before the population could exit. After the last of the Earths human population had left, a few of every known animal species was collected by the robots and sent to numerous zoos in the new planet. Shortly after they all had entered the planet, several large meteors crashed into Earth wiping out major cities and killing many people that were left behind. The doorways that weren't destroyed had been deactivated by the robots. The temple in the Yucatan was intact and operational, to be used for checking on Earths status. All the people entering the planet were amazed and delighted with their new home, some experiencing freedom for the first time. Some political problems needed to be solved; a few former leaders of countries didn't like Al and Beth running things, but were pleased with their control of the robots and accepted the situation as is. Beth announced that the planet needed a name and that there would be a contest to name it; the winner would receive a big prize.

CHAPTER 6
UTOPIA

A lot of great names were entered in the contest, but the winning name chosen was 'Utopia", a fitting name that truly described the planet. The winner received a 30 day trip around the solar system visiting other planets and a stay at a very plush hotel and gambling casino that is in orbit around Utopia. Back on Utopia, Al and Beth invited all former leaders of countries a seat at the long table in the conference room. Al and Beth presided over the meeting with their trusted friends by their sides, the ones that traveled with them initially to the temple. All their friends except the law enforcement person who betrayed their trust; he was lucky to get into Utopia. In the meeting they were all told that they were in a true utopian world, food, water, clothing and shelter is available to everyone at no cost. No one has to work but if specific services are performed than credits will be issued allowing access to the many entertainments that are available. Order is maintained by the robots; they have no emotions and will treat any violators swiftly and without remorse and treat all people as being equal. They were told to tell all their former countrymen that if they followed all the rules that life here would be easy, uncomplicated and enjoyable. All terrorists and people with hate and prejudice had better put it away as long as they are on Utopia; shipping violators back to Earth is not out of the question. They were told that a team is being put together to design a device that would orbit Earth and remove the dust cloud that is causing the devastation. If successful, it could shorten the time considerably when return would be possible. Al said, "When we get back, robots will assist in the rebuilding of Earth's devastated cities. Beth and I dream of both planets being co joined in utopian splendor, where the principles used successfully in Utopia are utilized on Earth; with no wars, no hunger, no genocide and all people living together in peace. We are acutely aware that we have a race of aliens to thank for our salvation and therefore have our leading medical researchers working on ways to retrieve their DNA and bring back their race as it was in their former glory."

CHAPTER 7
TWENTY YEARS LATER

Al and Beth controlled the robots and established peace and harmony in Utopia for twenty years. The research to retrieve the alien DNA was unsuccessful; the aliens had mutated considerably over their generations to the point were no recovery was possible. Utopia must be careful not to fall into the trap of complacency as the aliens did. Pictures of the aliens from their vast library showed a striking resemblance to the Mayans; it's possible that some of their research may have worked.

In the twentieth year of habitation by earthlings on Utopia a device was manufactured that could orbit Earth and vacuum the dust cloud around the planet. Hundreds would be needed to complete the task. The first ones built were sent to earth through the Yucatan temple and they worked well. Mass production followed and after one year the results proved very successful with an abundance of sunlight hitting the planet. The planet began to rejuvenate and dormant plants and seedlings started to sprout.

Al and Beth called for a meeting in the conference room and Al said, "People, it's time for you, who want to return to Earth to make your plans. Regal will instruct his robots to assist you in any way that you may require." In the twenty plus years that passed, a new philosophy had emerged with the younger generation that was ingrained in them of the Utopian life style; they were sure to bring that back to Earth.

CHAPTER 8
THE TALIBAN

Over twenty years ago when the last of Earths' people left, The Taliban elected to stay; they retreated to under ground cities that they had built ten years earlier. Their plan at the time was to instigate a nuclear holocaust that they alone could survive. Their plans changed a little with the meteors substituting for nuclear weapons. During their under ground stay, they stockpiled nuclear weapons preparing for the day when the Earth was ready for inhabitation. Many of the Arabs and terrorists joined them and they were clever enough to send spies along with the people leaving Earth.

When the people started inhabiting the Earth, the Taliban, alerted by their spies, sent missiles with nuclear war heads at them destroying any chance to rebuild and causing chaos. The sole doorway to the planets remained intact in the Yucatan protected by its force field and cloaking ability; the robot remained as a silent sentinel.

Al and Beth stopped emigration to consider the situation of Taliban aggression. They called a meeting together of all past Admirals, Generals and war tactics specialists.

Addressing the group Beth said, "We need a plan of war to retaliate against the Taliba back on Earth. Al and I have told Regal and his robots to work with you people that we have designated and they will respond to your commands. We are at a big disadvantage because the Taliban have been stockpiling weapons and planning for this day for years. We have faith that these obstacles can be overcome. We are starting production on a craft that is provided with weapons that can discharge a lightening bolt of electricity that kills all electronics and hits with devastating force. We will try to utilize any ships, aircraft and systems that are still recoverable. We have many people who have commanded them before. Good luck and go get them."

The war continued for two years at the cost of many lives; the Utopians were able to get a lot of old equipment running and the aircraft carriers were very helpful in providing a movable base of operation. The Admirals and Generals knew their stuff and slowly began to overcome the Taliban. Finally the Taliban, knowing that they could not win, let off a barrage of nuclear missiles to all parts of the Earth which filled the Earth with radiation and devastation that would make many parts of the Earth uninhabitable for many years. The Taliban retreated to their under ground cities knowing to follow them would be folly. No attempt was made to follow them but their entrances were sealed leaving them to the fate that they had created. The nuclear onslaught made the Earth uninhabitable in the great cities and in other areas that could have been viable for building.

CHAPTER 9
REBUILDING.

New cities were started in unlikely places like deserts, underwater, in the sky and in the North and South Poles. The war had unleashed global warming that melted the ice at the poles and flooded a lot of seacoast and all of Florida. Al and Beth finished their lives in Utopia but not before they saw a great returning and rebuilding of Earth. The new leaders controlled the robots and many years of peace followed in both planets. Finally one day in the future the entrance to the under ground cities was opened.

The people that entered were shocked to see the hell that the Taliban had made for themselves. They encountered mutants with distorted features and a society completely in disarray; they had consumed all of their food and were eating people as they died. Their numbers were far less than original and their weapons useless. Their leaders had killed themselves or were murdered and consumed by the people. They were offered freedom, unhampered, to the surface but quickly came back; they couldn't stand the light. Food was brought in for them but they preferred eating the dead. Finally they were left alone to their fate, a grim one at best. The Arabs that did not follow them initially lived a wonderful life in the true Muslim religious meaning of love and peace. The temple in the Yucatan became a shrine for Al and Beth; their bodies were entombed in it. The doorway to the universe remained active in the temple along with many others that were constructed for travel back and forth to Utopia.

CHAPTER 10
A REVERSE EXODUS

Millions of years in the future humans will evolve and look different than they did in Al and Beth's time. The planets will continue to evolve; however Utopia, being a very old planet in a very old Solar System will reach the end of its existence. The sun will finally use up its fuel and explode into a Super Nova. Great waves of fire will head for Utopia and its whole solar system. The Earth will return the great service provided for them millions of years ago by allowing millions of people on Utopia to escape to Earth. Utopia will be reduced to a burnt cinder; a fate that Earth will share in the far future and its people also unless they can find another planet to jump to.

THE ETERNAL TRAVELER

A being was created during the early creation of the universe. It evolved over the initial billions of years during the early development and expansion of the universe. Its DNA reached its maximum advancement and its complexity provided it with the ability to transform itself into pure energy and back to solid material at will. It was one of many during its time, but the only one, apparently, to survive and obtain eternal life. It can't die and its computer intelligence mind contains all the knowledge in the universe. In energy form it is able to traverse the universe in zero time while billions of years pass for the rest of the universe. Not content at being the only intelligent being to witness the miracle of the universe it searches for life on planets throughout the universe. One planet in a likely solar system showed great promise. Its sun was just the right distance from the planet to support life; its size was perfect to hold a breathable atmosphere for inhabitants. The being set down on the planets surface in its solid form and noticed that the inhabitants were very primitive and hostile. It changed his appearance to mix in with the primates. It examined their kind and decided that a boost to their development was possible by instilling them with some of its DNA. It left the planet at the speed of light with the intention of returning in the future.

After traveling around the planets galaxy looking for other prospects it returned to the planet. Only a year had passed for the traveler but 40 million years had passed on the planet. The being was delighted at the advanced civilization it encountered on the planet. The inhabitants had mastered science and mathematics and were well along in space exploration. The being decided to spend some time on the planet and to that end took on the look and form of the inhabitants. The being adopted the name Al Powers and blended into the planet's society. He forged papers giving him credentials as a PHD in Science, Chemistry, Cosmology and Astronomy; a lot to believe but he could back up every bit and a lot more. He joined an experimental group of scientists in a branch of the government that worked on top secret projects. He soon dazzled all with his knowledge and ability to solve intricate problems. Being careful not to advance their knowledge before they were capable of dealing with it; he nudges them forward. They had already explored their solar system and were preparing for the next step, possibly to another solar system. They were looking at a distant star that was 50 light years away and were preparing to send dedicated astronauts to it by freezing them to prolong their life for the journey. Al headed a department that considered alternate ways to travel great distances in space time. Al approached the Project Manager, John Adam and said, "I've been studying an alternate approach at reaching that distant solar system and I think I have a much better way to get there." John said, "I know you're pretty smart but there can't be any other way with our present technology." "Al said you're right but I have some new technology for you to look at." Al new all about the distant star and its solar system because he had just come from there. The inhabitants had also been boosted by Al, but were at least a millennium behind this planet in evolution. Al said, "I've completed calculations on the design of a time wave generating machine that will make the journey possible in one year." Al went over the calculations with John but John couldn't understand the advanced math. He called in a team of top scientists who were barely able to understand it but agreed they could not find anything wrong with the concept. Ultimately he was given the funding and resources to have the machine built. A concerted effort ensued culminating in a machine built and tested that could do the job. Al designed a telescope that was capable of seeing life on the distant planet. The concept was a revolutionary design in reflective optics. Using the telescope, Al spotted advanced life on the planet. This did not make sense; his boost to their evolution should not have shown these results for centuries to come. The Astronauts took off and after more than a year there was no information from them. They should have returned by this time. Viewing carefully through his telescope he spotted many space ships heading toward them. He went to the main seat of the government and addressed the president and said, "Sir an invasion is heading this way and will be attacking this planet in 5 months." The president said, "I'd like to believe you in lieu of all the scientific breakthroughs you have achieved but recent information has been reported to me that you forged all your academic credentials. Our military guard is here to arrest you for perjury." Al said, "I wouldn't do that if I were you." At which point he froze all the guards and turned into his pure energy form. The president sat down completely awed, and said, "Who or what are you?" Al said, "I'm what you see, pure energy. I come from the early beginning of the universe. I greatly boosted your evolutionary development millions of years ago to what you are today. We are definitely related and I have come back to your planet to help and protect you." Al returned to solid form and told the president that what he has seen is for his eyes only. The president composed himself and said, "It all makes sense now that's why your superior intelligence and creative ability is beyond our technical knowledge.

What can we do to prepare for the impending invasion?" Al said, "First, Mr. President, appoint me as you're science advisor; reporting only to you, then give me free control to handle the situation." The president said, "I'll advise my generals." Al then directed contractors in the building of a giant force field that would be impossible to penetrate. They finished the equipment barely in time as the attacking forces arrived. Finding their effort completely thwarted the attacking forces tried to negotiate. They claimed that they were invaded by their astronauts and they were forced to kill them to protect themselves. The president refuted their claim stating that they were on a friendly exploration mission hoping to find intelligent life. The President said, "Your action in killing innocent people is considered an act of war. I suggest you turn around and go home; don't come back until you're ready to make restitution." They turned around and left; the situation being completely diffused by the force field. Al told the president that he would be leaving the planet now and that he had left them with enough technology to take them far into the future. He said, "Tell no one of me, I'll be back someday to see how you progressed." Al left the planet at the speed of light wondering how the attacking forces had progressed so far.

Al stopped off at the warring planet to find out what had happened. He was amazed to see that they were in the middle of a nuclear war with other parts of the planet. Using the same name and sex as before he changed to solid form and confronted the leaders of the warring nations. He asked, " Why are you fighting with each other and why did you attack a distant planet?" The leaders said," You told us to, in exchange for the advanced technology you gave us." Al said, "I never gave you any advanced knowledge." The leaders said, "If it wasn't you then it was someone like you with the same powers." Al was surprised for a minute until he realized that their must be another like himself that evolved and survived. He told the leaders that the war was over and he cancelled the advanced knowledge they obtained and returned them to the correct place in their evolution. He left the planet with a new mission, to find his alien brother and stop his crazy interference.

He traveled to another planet that he had helped along only to find the burnt out charred remains of a planet. He arrived too late to save it. Extremely worried about the other planets he helped along; he sped out in curved space time to the next planet that he had helped. He arrived in time to catch his alien brother in the act of pushing the inhabitants into war. They confronted each other in solid form and Al said, "Where did you come from and why are you trying to hurt these people?" His alien brother said, "I came from the same place as you; you left before you had a chance to see that I existed also. I had been trying to find you for millions of years. Finally I got tired of looking and tired of being alone. I stir up these natives to add a little excitement to my existence." Al said, "What's wrong with you? Don't you have any compassion for these people?" His alien brother said, "No more than I would for any insect." Al said, "You're sick and evil and no brother of mine. I advise you to get off this planet and stop interfering with my work. At that the alien brother left laughing saying stop me if you can.

Al corrected the problems and left the planet chasing after his evil brother. He caught up to him as he was heading for another planet that had been evolved by Al. Al said, "Who do you think you are treating people that way, God?" The alien said, "Why not look at the supreme power we have." Al said, "You keep thinking that and God will punish you and if he doesn't, I will." They started toward each other and clashed in their energy form. The coming together of two energy forms caused a catastrophic explosion that could be heard across the universe. Each time they came at each other they were repelled many light years across the universe. Finally their fight took them into an area of the universe where there was absolutely no material.

[115]

As they continued to clash, pieces of energy would break off and compress into suns and planets from the force of gravity. The more they clashed the more material would fill the void. Without realizing it, they were becoming weaker and smaller. Finally they were reduced to nothing but wisps of energy trapped in several galaxies that they had created. Al's last thought was, " at least I have rid the world of evil energy."

FAR SIGHT

John Louis Cristos is a second generation American. His father came over from Greece, met a nice French American girl and settled in New England. John was born a year later and grew up with inherited ability for inventing. He worked for many companies that used his talent to reward their own agenda and to give credit to others that they favored. One day he got some bad news that his grandfather had died. He traveled to Greece for the funeral and was surprised at all the attention his grandfather's death was getting. Top government people, many friends and associates and worldwide news people were there. He learned that his grandfather was loved and respected by many people. His grandfather was an inventor and had produced numerous devices that were instrumental in advancing medicine in this century. To John's surprise, his grandfather left his entire estate to him; including all royalties from inventions. His grandfather had been watching John's progress and had been very proud of him. He knew John was following in his footsteps and wanted him to be financially free to pursue his creations.

John decided to do exactly as his grandfather had wished. He quit his job and prepared to work on his lifelong dream of building a super microscope. He purchased an old warehouse building and installed security devices and fortified the inside with impregnable construction. He set up a laboratory with the latest equipment needed for his tasks. The design involved the use of gamma rays that required an immense amount of power. What he could acquire from the electric company was marginal at best, but he decided to proceed anyway.

John's wife and son lived in a comfortable home that he built to be close to his family before his mother and father were killed in an auto accident.

John and his wife divorced after the death of John's parents. His wife claimed that he was a different man after their death and impossible to live with. John buried himself in his work after his parent's death and was never home. John left her independently wealthy. John's son, Homer, was finishing his last year of graduate school for mechanical and electrical engineering. John had graduated from the same college many years before and was pleased with his son's achievement

No one was allowed into the laboratory; equipment coming in had to be left on the ground floor entrance elevator and from there brought up to the lab, under close scrutiny. The super microscope machine was massive with gamma ray coils in place, computer hook up and viewing screen. John's concern about power consumption forced him to provide four levels of power input. All this effort took several months until finally he was ready for a trial run. He turned on the machine and noted that the gamma ray coils consumed more power than he had anticipated. The computer screen showed the area just below the viewing tube. He slowly moved the view downward, past molecules, then to the atomic structure. The movement at the atomic level was so intense that he could not get a clear picture. He shut down, being very frustrated and disappointed that all his efforts might be in vain. He was at a standstill and almost ready to give up; he left the building to attend his son's graduation from college. Later at a graduation party, he was told by his son that he would like to go into business with him. John looked at his son in anguish and said, "I'd like nothing better but I'm not having any success with my new designs." His son, Homer, said, "Show me the operation, maybe I can help." John brought him to the Lab and explained the operation of the super microscope.

Homer said, "Wow, this is a great design, what's the problem?" John turned on the machine and showed Homer the point of failure. Homer said, "Dad you've worked so hard to get this far that your missing the obvious solution." "John said, "What do you mean?" Homer said, "All we have to do is to create an area of absolute zero temperature and all activity will either slow down or stop. I'll design a refrigeration system into the machine that will lower the temperature in the viewing area." John said, "I think you've got the answer; go ahead and build it; cost is no problem." Several weeks later the equipment was ready and in place. They turned on the machine and as Homer had predicted the action slowed down and they could view the atomic structure. The nucleus was plainly shown as well as the electrons. John zoomed into the electron and saw that it was made up of several particles as scientist's had predicted. He pointed the viewer tube at one particular particle but did not have enough power to see it clearly. John said, "Let's go to the next power level." Homer switched to half power and they were both astonished at what they saw just before all the power died. John shut down the machine and said to his son, "Do you believe what we saw?" Homer said, "Maybe we were dreaming." John said, "No we both saw it; we need more power to confirm it."

After being shut down for lack of power, Homer told his father that he could design a power system that could provide all the power needed. It will operate independent from local power and run on ordinary fuel. John said, "Go for it son, it looks like we have got ourselves a company." When John took his son home that day, his ex-wife said, "Where have you been with my son?" When John told her that they were in business together doing research and development, she was delighted.

Weeks later, the power system was completed, tested and performing as expected. John said, "Well son here we go." He turned on the super mike and zoomed down to the electron particle as he did before. He switched to half power and there was absolutely no doubt about it; the viewer screen revealed a small universe like the one they were in. They saw tiny galaxies and what looked like solar systems. John said, "Homer, go to three quarter power; there it is a clear view of the galaxies, but we'll have to go to full power to get a clearer view of the solar systems." At full power they saw a clear view of the solar systems and orbiting planets. They also saw area's of Nova explosions and probable black holes. John said, "Son, do you realize what this means? This little universe is typical of all the particles and that there are billions of universes with atomic structures and on to infinity." Homer poured the champagne as they celebrated their success. After reflecting for a while, John said, "I don't think we should reveal our findings to the world; it could cause chaos around the planet." Homer agreed and said, "Where do we go from here? I wonder if our universe is also one of those electron particles in a larger universe." John said, "I think we can reverse our design and build a super telescope that can see beyond the universe."

They both decided to give it a try. After many months of design and fabrication, they finally had the machine that could do the job. They fortified the top of the building and placed the machine on a retractable track. They switched to one quarter power and were able to view the edge of the universe. They switched to one half power only to find that the universe seemed to be just as far away. They tried full power with the same results. They shut down the system to discuss the problem. John said, "We seem to have come to an impasse; the universe seems to be expanding faster than

[122]

light speed. We need to speed up our light source faster than light." Homer said, "Einstein said that couldn't be done." However, I have some scientist friends that might have an answer." John said, "Be careful not to reveal our equipment status." Homer said, "Ok dad, don't worry." He spent some time with his friends and after playing, what if, games at the intellectual level; he obtained theoretical information on how it might be possible to go beyond the universe.

Later, when he got together with his dad, Homer said, "My friends said that it might be possible to leave the universe through a gigantic black hole in space." John said, "It's worth a try. Let's aim at the gigantic black hole in the center of our galaxy and see what happens," Back in the lab, they turned on the system, moved it forward on the track and aimed at the center of the galaxy. They moved the viewing tube toward the black hole and saw many black holes whirling around the gigantic black hole. As they got closer, they saw a fantastic amount of material including suns being sucked into the black hole. When they were about to enter the black hole, the computer screen went blank; apparently no pictures were coming back. John said, "Well, that's what I expected; light can't escape from a black hole." Homer said, "That's true, dad, but x-rays and radiation can escape and the computer is picking up something. Let's continue at full power and see what happens." After several minutes, they shut down the super telescope and down loaded the computer data onto a disc. They were not able to decipher the data but they knew something was there.

Homer took the disc to his scientist friends and asked them if they could decipher the data. Weeks later he got a call from his friends to come over and see what they had for him. When he arrived, his friend said, "What kind of a joke were you playing on us? This data shows a phony distant universe revolving around a hugh atomic nucleus. We know you must have created this picture to play a crude joke on us. You wasted a lot of our valuable time trying to decipher the data." Homer apologized and scooped up all the information and left.

When Homer showed his father the information from the data, he jumped for joy. John said, "It worked we were able to see beyond the universe; this proves our universe is in an electron particle in a much larger universe and that there are billions of universe's like ours." Later, after much celebration, they decided to set up manufacturing of microscopes and telescopes superior to anything available to date but without the super capability of the experimental models. This would bring in needed funds to continue further experimenting. The plan was to work on an idea that John had to explore the electron particle universe.

ONE PLACE OR THE OTHER

Jake Giovanni lived in East Boston all his life. He quit school in the ninth grade lured by fast money selling dope to hooked customers. By the time he was thirty years old he had joined the mob and was considered a small time hustler by law enforcement people. He was tall and thin and not very well groomed but his zeal attracted some women. Whenever he made a little money, he would quickly spend it on gambling, booze and women.

One day, as he was traveling along in his red convertible, he attempted to light a cigarette while going 80 miles per hour. He dropped the lighter in his lap and while attempting to put it out; he swerved off of the road and crashed into a large oak tree. He opened his eyes a little while later, saw his predicament and jumped out of the car. He looked down the road and spotted a gambling casino. He started for it hoping to get some help. When he arrived at the casino he was impressed by the huge ornate building and couldn't remember seeing it before. The attendant welcomed him and said, "Good evening sir, welcome to the Blazing Casino, we offer you $100 in free chips; come in and try your luck, food and drink is complimentary." Jake couldn't refuse that offer; after the crash he needed a good stiff drink. He sat down and drank and ate until he was completely satisfied. He said to the casino manager, "I've crashed my car down the road and need help." The manager said, "Don't worry about it we'll take care of it for you." Jake couldn't believe the hospitality and said, "I thank you very much, where are the crap tables?" The manager led him to the crap tables, handed him a pair of dice and wished him good luck. Jake's luck was phenomenal, he couldn't lose. Soon he attracted a crowd; everyone was playing for him to win. A pretty young women came along side of him and said, "I'm here to give you good luck, break the bank and you win me too." Jake's excitement was heightened as he continued to win. Finally the house closed down the table claiming Jake had broken the bank. The manager approached Jake and said, "If you will stay over and play tomorrow, giving us a chance to get even, we will offer you the presidential suite for you and your girl. We will also include a brand new car to replace your crashed one." Jake accepted the offer and proceeded to the suite with his new girl friend on his arm. In the suite Jake learned that his girl friend's name was Babs. She told him that she loved a winner. After exhaustive sex, Jake fell asleep bewildered by his unbelievable good luck. Jake woke up early in the morning, raring to go. He couldn't wake Babs up so he decided to take a drive in his new car before breakfast. Down the road his car suddenly stopped next to an old man. The man gestured that he get out of his car. Jake said, "What do you want old man?" The old man said, "Did you enjoy yourself last night?" Jake said, "Yes what business is it of yours?" The old man said, "It is my business because you died in that car crash and what you enjoyed last night I can offer you for ever." Jake got angry, told the old man where to go and headed back to the car crash scene. When he got back to where he thought the casino should be, it was no longer there. He thought to himself that maybe the old man was right and I am really dead. He went to the car crash scene and saw his mangled body and sat down holding his head in horror realizing he was really dead. He thought that the old man must be an angel from god offering me a good deal. He went back to where the old man was standing; he got out of the car and apologized for telling him where to go. He said, you must be an angel from god offering me a good deal in my after life."

The old man said, "You're partly right I am an angel, a dark angel, and god did not send me; also, I live where you told me to go." Jake said, "You mean that offer you made me wasn't from heaven?" The old man said, "No, it's the other place." Jake said, "Oh! But it did seem like a pretty good place. How do I know that heaven isn't better?" The old man replied, "You're free to try, but if heaven doesn't accept you, I wont be able to make you the same offer as before. These places are in big demand and I will have to offer it to the next in line. The next place we have to offer you is not so nice; it's more like a war zone. If you go to heaven, try to get in and fail; all I will have for you is the next in line, as I described. I have other places but they're a lot worse." Jake said, "I can't see why they wont accept me; I never killed anybody and I did take care of my mother. The rest of my life wasn't so good but I don't think I deserve to go to hell."

Jake left the old man and went down the road and stopped at heavens gate. Another old man was there who introduced himself as St. Peter. Jake said, "I'm Jake Giovanni, I assume I'm at heavens gate. What's it like in there?" St. Peter said, "It's blissfully peaceful in here, no wars, no violence, and just serene paradise." Jake said, "It sounds kind of boring." St. Peter said, "Some have thought that and went to the other place." Jake said, "I Think I'd like to get in here; what's the chances?" St. Peter said, "Let me check the great book. I see that your life history is nothing to be proud of." However, one thing is necessary before we can even consider you. Do you see that man over there?" Jake said, "Yes I do." St. Peter said, "That's the big boss, no one gets by without his approval." Jake said, "I never believed in that story; it really boils down to Santa Claus and Christmas that big business uses to get the suckers to buy their junk."

Take all those Catholic Priests, with their holier than thou attitude, that turned out to be pedophiles." St. Peter said, "Yes, they sinned very badly and hurt a lot of people. But they're in here because they believed and asked for forgiveness. It took a while to get them in here and they're doing some menial tasks to humble them. In about one thousand years they may retain full status." Jake said, "Well, in that case, I believe and I ask forgiveness." St. Peter said, "I'll talk it over with the boss." He came back a little later and said, "The boss said no, because you're not sincere and to try again in about a thousand years." Jake said, "All right, this place looks boring anyway." Jake went back to the other place, confronted the old man and said. "I can't get in up there, what have you got for me here?" The old man said, "I warned you before; you've lost your place to Luigi Guglio." Jake said, "What, he was a lot worse than me; he even killed people." The old man said, "Yes. But he didn't try to get into the other place. He accepted my first offer." Jake had no choice but to accept his fate. He went to his new car to drive to his place and saw that it had turned into an old junk. He drove up to a casino in the new place. He entered the building with no greeting and no offer of money. He went to the crap table and lost at every roll of the dice. An ugly old hag came to his side and said, "Hi Jake." He said, "Do I know you?" She said, "I'm Babs." He said, "What happened to you?" She said, "When you refused the first offer, I was blamed for failing at my task." Jake left the casino and saw that his car had been stolen. He had no recourse when he found out that there were no police anywhere. He walked down town and got mugged by a group of guys. They beat him badly when they discovered that he had no money. He thought, "I'm starting to believe; I hope I can last a thousand years.

Walking along in a daze and bleeding badly, he bumped into a guy that was in the same mob when he was alive.

Jake said, "Mario what are you doing here?" Mario said, "I could ask you the same question." Jake said, "Ya, we both got what we deserved." Mario said, "Come with me, we have got the mob together and manage to survive by sticking together." The rest of the gang was glad to see him. They showed him the ropes and gave him his place in the hierarchy. Later, he ran into his sister's kid, Lance. Jake said, "What are you doing in this god forsaken place." Lance said, "I followed in your footsteps, Uncle Jake, and when you died, I took over your place in the mob." Jake thought to himself, "I've got a lot to answer for; I didn't realize the bad example that I was setting for others." For the first time, he felt genuinely sorry for what he done in his life. He decided that the least he could do would be to protect his dear sister's child.

They were both invited to a mob meeting. When they got there Jake noticed that Luigi Guglio was running the meeting and in charge. Jake approached Mario and said, "You had a good deal that the old man gave you in place of me; why did you leave?" Luigi said, "I tried to take over in there and the old man didn't like it, but I'm taking over here, any objections." Jake said, "Nope, it's all yours." Later, Jake was confronted by the old man who said, 'How would you like your first choice place, I have an opening now." Jake said, "No thanks, I want to stay here to keep an eye on my nephew and keep him out of trouble." The old man said, "Your making a big mistake, I won't ask you again." Jake said, "I know but I'm not thinking of myself." The old man left grumbling to himself.

Jake stepped outside, and suddenly he was in front of St. Peter who said, "Jake, the boss is very impressed with your actions in that other place and would like to give you another chance, what do you say?" Jake said, "I'm really sorry for my life and truly believe but I can't leave my nephew alone in that place." St. Peter said, "We understand that you feel responsible for your nephew and need to watch over him. If at any time you feel you want to come in here, just say the words, "I'm ready lord" and you'll be here." Back in the other place, Jake stopped his nephew from committing a crime that was ordered by Luigi. He told his nephew that the life they had lived was wrong and that he should mend his ways. At first Lance was confused but slowly began to change his ways by Jakes example. Jake told him, "Don't do anything Luigi tells you to do; he is evil and loves this existence, but you are not and there is a chance for your salvation." They both suffered at the hands of Luigi but stayed committed to a better existence. Finally, Jake said, "Lord I'm ready." Immediately he arrived in heaven and to his surprise Lance was with him.

The old man in the other place had a devil of a time dealing with the loss of two souls.

CPSIA information can be obtained at www.ICGtesting.com
Printed in the USA
LVOW062129270112

265901LV00001B/315/P